THE LIGHT HE FOUND

CAITLIN LEDGER

Contents

1

CHAPTER 1

K ELLAN
Age 9

My eyes are glued to the TV. I'm eating my sandwich at the dining table. I can't take my gaze off the news aired on TV right now. It's the national headline.

There was a bank robbery, and the CCTV caught the bad guys shooting the employees.

I wince as the sound of gun shooting and people's scream echo. Even though it's coming from the TV, it feels real. I'm suddenly losing my appetite for breakfast.

"That sounds disgustingly cruel and barbaric," Inez, my sister who just turned seven this month, complains from across the table.

We're having breakfast together, but she has chosen the seat with her back facing the TV, just like usual, to avoid seeing some horrible news she can't bear to witness. Unfortunately, it's always around this time that Dad's friend turns on the news every morning.

The sound of footsteps catches my attention, and I find mom walking down the stairs while speaking on the phone.

"We'll be there in no time, sweetheart." A smile touches her lips while she's listening to the voice from the other side of the line.

I know who she's speaking to. It must be my older brother, Jaxon. "Don't worry. All of us will be there to support you. Everyone is excited and can't wait to watch your first karate championship. Just listen to your instructor and take a deep breath. We'll be there shortly."

They talk a bit more before mom hangs up. She sighs, and I can see the excitement on her face.

Jaxon left earlier for the karate championship with his instructor to get warmed up before the competition. Inez and I will go there with mom to support him. I hope that dad can make it as well, but he's a very busy person.

I'm excited and nervous for Jaxon because this is his very first championship. At the age of 13, Jaxon has been one of the best karate students in his martial arts school. He's expected to win a medal in this competition.

Mom kisses my cheek as soon as she arrives at the dining table. Then she approaches Inez and does the same. She's glowing with happiness, but then her smile disappears as soon as she sees the TV.

"Fenrir," she snaps, glaring at the said man. "Again? I told you to not show such violence in front of my children. Please, can't you at least switch the channel to something else?"

Fenrir shifts his attention to mom. "Sorry. I got carried away while following the case." He changes the channel, which is now showing the news about drug trafficking.

Mom sighs, and I can see that she's still irritated. I don't know why mom seems to hate him. Fenrir is actually a nice person. People would think that he looks intimidating on first impression -- with his piercing dark eyes and a cut on his left cheek that makes him look like a gangster in movies -- but he's actually fun to hang out with.

Sometimes, he likes to play games with me and Jaxon, like letting us aim our water guns at his shooting target board.

He once showed me his real gun and let me touch it.

Fenrir and some other close friends of dad's hang around here in our house very often. They usually spend a night here every other day. Our house has plenty of rooms, so there's always space for everyone.

Some people even call our house a mansion because we have more than 20 rooms. I've heard some of them also say that it's like some kind of 'base'.

I don't know the details of dad's job, but I know for sure that he makes a lot of money. He's the founder of an organization.

Dad rushes downstairs, catching mom's attention. He's dressed in casual attire and wearing his black jacket, which is a good thing. He usually wears his suit before going to negotiation, so it means that he's not going to work today.

Mom looks pleased with the sight, a sign that dad is going to come with us to watch Jaxon's karate match.

"Have you finished your breakfast?" Dad greets me and Inez when he arrives downstairs. His gaze then darts to the TV. "Look there," he speaks to us in a fatherly tone. "Look at those guys over there trafficking drugs. They're the bad guys. Our job is to not become like them. Our job is to put them in their place. Understood?"

Inez and I nod in understanding. While mom always tries to not contaminate us with all things evil, dad prefers to show us both sides -- the good and the evil -- while making sure to guide us to choose the right path.

"Magnus." Fenrir stands up from the couch and strides toward dad's office. "Can we talk for a while?" he asks in a serious tone.

Dad stays on his spot while mom shakes her head in disagreement.

"Please, not now," mom begs. "He's waiting."

Judging from the way Fenrir spoke, he and dad are going to discuss an important work. And they always take a long time when they talk about work.

"Magnus," Fenrir calls, already inside dad's office with the door wide open for him to follow. "It's about the case you asked about yesterday."

Magnus is not dad's real name, and I've heard that Fenrir isn't his real name either. I don't know why they use all those fake names.

Dad sighs and gives mom an apologetic look. "Please give me a moment. It won't take long. I promise."

Mom watches in disbelief as dad enters his office and closes the door behind him. She sighs in frustration and takes a seat beside Inez. She caresses Inez's hair, telling us to be patient while waiting for dad to finish the discussion with Fenrir.

Only a minute passes after the door is closed, but the next thing we hear is them shouting at each other. I can't hear the words clearly, but it's obvious that both of them are furious.

I even think that they're going to kill each other because I can hear the sound of the furniture inside the room being toppled and crashed. I just hope that I won't hear any gunshots.

Inez jumps in her seat every time a loud voice reaches her ears.

"Come on," mom says, helping Inez stand up. Her eyes are telling me to do the same.

I follow suit, heading toward the car which is already waiting for us in the driveway. Mom opens the door for me and Inez to sit at the back. Our driver, Tristan, is already behind the wheel, but mom doesn't get into the car.

Instead, she walks a few steps away and pulls out a cigarette with her shaking hand. She always edges away when she's nervous, as though she doesn't want us to see such weakness.

No matter how hard she tries to hide it, I know it when mom is scared. I know it when she's feeling sad, when she's in pain.

I shift my attention to Inez, who's shaking beside me. "Will dad be okay?" she stutters.

I put my palms on her shoulders, trying to calm her. She looks up at me with her big emerald eyes. They're filled with tears and fear.

I hate to see Inez cry. I hate to see mom cry. I want to learn martial arts like Jaxon does so that I can protect them too when someone tries to harm them.

"Of course, he'll be okay," I say, believing in my own words.

I haven't seen any other man as strong as dad. That's why he's been the leader of this organization. Fenrir might be his advisor, but dad is called the destroyer. No one gets in his way.

However, I can see that Inez is still afraid, so I decide to distract her mind.

"Let's play Sticks," I say, starting with one finger out on each of my hands.

Inez stares at me, probably still debating if she wants to play this finger-counting game with me.

"Come on." I smirk, making her sigh.

She pulls one finger out of each hand too.

"Your turn first," I say, giving her a head start.

She taps my hand, and we start playing. She wins the first round, but surprisingly, she pouts.

"You gave me the chance to start first, so it was obvious that I was going to win," she says matter-of-factly. "Now, it's your turn to start first."

I notice that her mind is already distracted, which is good. This time, I take a head start, but when she wins again, she groans.

"That's not fair," she exclaims. "You purposely took the wrong step so that I could win."

I laugh, and she does too. It's such a relief to see her happy face again.

The funny thing is that we always play this game like this, but she never gets bored of it. I think she enjoys being spoiled.

Movement from the house startles us. A huge relief washes over me when I see dad storming in our direction.

"Let's go," he urges.

After mom and dad gets into the car, Tristan immediately starts driving.

2

CHAPTER 2

K ELLAN
Age 9

"Put your seatbelt on," mom reminds me and Inez in a worried tone.

She's always being extra careful when it comes to us, but sometimes I wonder if there's something else that makes her paranoid all the time.

Inez and I obey her command, fastening our seatbelts. The three of us are sitting at the back with Inez in the middle of us while dad is sitting in the front seat beside Tristan.

Mom's phone rings, and when she pulls it out, I can see Jaxon requesting a video call. She accepts the call, and we can see Jaxon already dressed in his karate uniform. He looks damn anxious, but his face brightens the moment he sees us all in the car.

"We're already on the way." Mom smiles at him, and her words make him sigh in relief.

Mom moves her phone so that Jaxon can have a closer look at me and Inez.

"Are you going to win the competition?" I challenge him in a lazy voice.

As expected, Jaxon smirks. "You'll see. I want you to see it for yourself. Can't wait to knock them out."

I chuckle. He's being cocky, but I like that confidence in him.

"Hey, Inez," he greets our sister cheerfully. "What gift do you want me to buy for you if I win the competition?"

Inez stares at him with a lost expression. "Will I get a gift?"

Jaxon grins widely. "Of course. If I win this championship, I'm going to get a lot of money, and I'll get you anything you want."

Inez squints, deep in thought. "Really?" Then she suddenly bursts into giggles. "If that's the case, I want a new headband."

This time, it's Jaxon's turn to stare at her with a stupid expression. "What? Just that?"

Inez nods enthusiastically.

"Really?" Jaxon asks in disbelief. "I can give you more."

"I just want a new pretty headband right now, and I can't think of anything else," Inez says truthfully with a big smile on her face.

Jaxon rubs the back of his head. "Well, if that's what you want..."

"What about me, huh?" I cut him off in an annoyed tone. "Will I not get anything?"

This sounds embarrassing, but I can't hide the fact that I feel slightly jealous. I always act like a cool brother to Inez, but when it comes to Jaxon, I sometimes act like a brat.

Jaxon tsks. "I knew that you would ask me for that, and that's why I didn't ask you. What do you have in mind, huh?"

"I want a horse," I say firmly, just for the sake of pissing him off.

"What the f--"

"Do you have any problem with that?" I ask. "You said that you would buy anything Inez wants, so that's my turn now. I want a horse," I emphasize the last sentence. "You better get that for me."

Jaxon scoffs, shaking his head. "There's no way that I'm getting you a horse. That's ridiculous. I'm not going to afford that. You can take any horse from dad's ranch if he allows you to. Why would I buy you a new horse?"

I scoff too, making it more obvious that he's getting on my nerves.

He rolls his eyes. "Fine, I'll get you a bicycle. How about that? But it shouldn't be expensive. I'll get you a cheap one."

"I don't need a bicycle," I bark.

"Geez, you're impossible." With that said, he ends the call. It makes me want to break something.

Mom and Inez laugh.

"Cocky bastard," I mutter. "It's not like he's going to win, anyway."

My conversation with Jaxon was silly, but that's the way we talk sometimes. That little bickering reminds me that no matter how horrible the situation we experienced with dad's job or his friends, it's just a small thing. Our family will always stick together, and it's all that matters.

When the car turns silent again, it's then I realize that dad hasn't spoken any word since we got into the car. He usually listens to our conversation, but today, it's different. He only pays attention to his phone, scrolling through the messages as if to confirm something.

I also realize that mom hasn't asked him any questions about what happened with Fenrir back home. Maybe they don't want to discuss it while still having me and Inez around.

Dad calls someone, who picks up the call after the first ring. "Are you positive about that?" he asks the person in such a low and dangerous tone that it makes the atmosphere in the car turn cold.

After the person gives him an answer, dad ends the call and hisses, "Fucking traitor."

His anger sends shivers down my spine. I've never seen dad so consumed in rage. Something awful must be happening.

The car suddenly takes a sharp turn, and that makes mom ask with urgency, "Why are we taking this road? We should go the other--"

"We're being followed," dad says.

The silence that follows after that sends chills through my body.

Inez and I exchange glances. Her face turns as white as paper. I hold her hand to comfort her while the car speeds off. We'd never been in a car with a speed this high before. Judging from Inez's expression, she's feeling nauseous and about to vomit.

Dad and Tristan don't have to share any words. They are both very aware of what's happening right now.

It seems that dad sees something from the rearview mirror because the next thing he does is pull out his gun, shocking us. My heart skips a beat, and I can hear Inez letting out a soft cry beside me.

Dad is going to shoot someone. Kill them, if necessary.

"No," mom objects. "Not in front of our children."

"I'm sorry," dad says. It's a firm apology because he's not going to change his mind. "I have to."

I watch as mom bites her lower lip, looking extremely pale. But she doesn't say anything anymore, knowing that dad has to protect us all.

In that split second, I see a van speeding toward us from the car window.

Look out!

I can't even say those words because the next thing I feel is a huge blow. I pull Inez closer to me and cover her while extreme pain stabs every nerve in my body.

Fear engulfs me, because despite feeling like dying, I'm still feeling the pain.

Until everything goes black.

3

Chapter 3

K ELLAN

Age 9

Every part of my body feels sore. I can't even move an inch.

It hurts. It hurts so much.

I try to move my head, but it feels like being attacked by a hammer.

I can hear faint whispers.

"He's just a little boy. Still very young," someone cries.

"What a tragedy."

Tragedy.

That one word makes me snap. I try to sit up but fail because of extreme pain. I want to scream, but what comes out of my mouth is a weak whimper.

I feel people rushing toward me, settling me back on the bed. My head hurts so much.

God, why is it so painful?

"Kellan." A man's voice echoes, close to me.

I know that voice. It's familiar.

I try to open my eyes, but it's so hard to do so. My eyelids flicker, and slowly, very slowly, I try to open my eyes. I'm sure that I've done that, but I keep failing. I can't see anything. It's total darkness.

"Kellan," the man speaks again, and I finally remember his voice. "It's me, Fenrir."

"F-Fenrir?" My voice is shaking. It sounds so weak and hoarse. "Where are you?"

"I'm right here beside you."

"Where?" My voice grows panicked. "Where are mom and dad? Where's Inez? I need to see them."

There's no response from him, which makes my heart race. I hear someone crying again, probably a nurse.

"Why are you not answering me?" I demand. "Where are they?"

To my horror, Fenrir sniffs. He's crying.

Fenrir never cries -- I just can't imagine that. And I don't like this.

"I'm sorry," he says in a sad tone. "I'm so sorry for what happened to your family."

I'm at a loss for words. Something wet rolls down my cheek, and I realize that I'm crying too.

All this time, I've always tried my best to not cry and be tough, but today, it's just too much. I can't do anything but cry.

"What are you talking about?" My voice is filled with anger. "Where are they?"

"Kellan." Fenrir takes a deep breath, as if he's trying to calm down too. "I did try to warn your dad, but he didn't listen. I knew that he was not supposed to get out of the house this morning. They had planned to kill him while he was on the way--" Fenrir stops short and curses under his breath.

I freeze.

They?

Who are they?

Are they the ones dad wanted to shoot earlier?

"What happened?" I raise my voice, becoming even more impatient. "What happened to him? What happened to mom and Inez? Why are you not bringing me to them?"

"I--" It seems that it's very hard for him to speak. "I don't think that you're in proper condition to know--"

"Fenrir!" I roar.

My chest is heaving up and down. I've never spoken to him like this, in such a commanding tone. But I've lost my patience. I want to know everything. I want somebody to take all this pain away.

Fenrir heaves a sigh. "A van coming from another road hit your father's car, crashing from the right side. Your mother and father died on the spot because they suffer the worst damage, as for Inez and the driver..."

I feel like the world around me crumble into pieces.

"They didn't make it either. You're the only one who survived. It's a miracle--"

"No." I shake my head in denial as tears stream down harder down my face. "No, it can't be true. You're lying. You're lying to me."

"Kellan--"

"I need to see them," I cry my heart out.

I can't move my body because of all these wounds. I hate to just sit here, shaking with fear.

"Just tell the doctor to do something to my eyes. I can't open it. Do something," I lash out.

"Kellan." Fenrir's voice is filled with sympathy. "You've already opened your eyes."

His words make me taken aback. It's already dark here, but I feel like I'm falling deeper into an endless pit.

"I'm sorry," he whispers. "It must be because of the injury from the crash. I can't see you like this, Kellan. I can't--" His voice is shaking as I feel him moving from his spot.

"Where's Jaxon?" It's the only question left to say as I feel my heart shatter into a million pieces.

Fenrir doesn't answer, so I cry again.

"Where is he? I need to see my brother."

I need to see Jaxon. He'll tell me that everything is alright. He'll tell me everything I need to know.

"He's here," Fenrir finally says. "But I don't think that the two of you can meet each other soon. He's not in a proper state either."

With that said, Fenrir leaves.

I wait, wait, and wait. But Jaxon still hasn't come yet.

The doctor visited me, but I didn't catch what he was saying. He didn't answer the question that had been lingering in my head. Instead, he said that I needed help first, as though he was waiting for a therapist before saying anything about my eyes.

It's when I hear shouting from outside the room that I come to my senses again. It's Jaxon.

"I need to see Kellan!" his loud voice echoes in the air, hysterical. "I need to see my brother!"

I can hear the fuss around him, as though the nurses are trying to put him back into another room, preventing him from seeing me.

"Jaxon, please," one of them says in a soothing voice. "Both of you are not in good condition right now. The help is coming. You can see your brother when both of you are in a good state. It's for his own good, and yours too."

I know what's going on. They're treating us like helpless kids, but what can we do to change that?

We are indeed kids.

"Jaxon," I stutter. "Jaxon!" I call him with all the energy left in my body.

"Let me go," he hisses to the people around him, and I can feel his movement when he rushes to the bed.

"Where are you?" I urge.

"I'm here." His hand grabs mine, and I can feel the warmth of his skin. I'm holding on to him like my life depends on him.

"Why can't I see you?" I sob.

I want to see. I really want to see. I hate this darkness.

"Why can't I see anything?"

Jaxon doesn't say anything, and I become even more restless. This is not the reaction that I expect from him.

"Why are you silent?" I ask.

The next thing I hear is his cry, and that makes my heart drop. I feel my eyes water again. My throat hurts so bad.

"Am I blind?" I whisper.

Jaxon sobs. "I'm sorry," he breaks down, tightening his hold on my hand. I can feel that he wants to hug me, but he can't do it because of how wounded I am. "I'm sorry, Kellan."

I don't know what I should do. Jaxon's hand is shaking as he cries with me. My heart feels like it doesn't exist anymore.

Why didn't I just die in the car crash?

Why am I still breathing?

Jaxon is holding my hand so tightly like I am his life, and maybe I am. If I'd died, what would have happened to him? He'll be all alone. Will he kill himself because of the pain?

"Where are mom and dad?" The question leaves my lips even thoughI might have already known the answer.

No. I want to hear it from Jaxon. Maybe he'll tell me that Fenrir was lying. I beg for him to do so. Mom, dad, and Inez must be somewhere in this hospital too, in another room.

"They're gone," Jaxon rasps, crushing my heart.

He breaks down again while I'm silently crying. I can't see anymore, but why can I still cry? I don't understand this world at all.

I wish that this is just a nightmare, but why does the pain feel so real?

"What about Inez?" I ask.

Jaxon's sobs break again. "She didn't make it either."

"No." I want to explode. "It can't be true. She was right in my arms. I was there protecting her. She's still alive, Jaxon. I was sure that she was still breathing."

I can't believe that Inez is gone too. My little sister is gone, the one I protected with my life when the crash happened.

Yet, Jaxon's pain is proof that everything is true. He's not lying. He's telling me the truth while holding on to me, just as tight as I am holding on to him. We never let go of each other's hand, as if the other would die if we did so.

Today is a nightmare that I won't be able to forget for the rest of my life.

I've lost mom, dad, and Inez.

And I'm blind.

4

— • —

CHAPTER 4

1 years later

Kellan, age 20 – Layla, age 19

L A Y L A

I kiss my grandma's cheek while she's swaying back and forth in her rocking chair. "I made a chicken soup for your breakfast and put it on the dining table. I gotta catch the bus."

A smile forms on my grandma's lips. Before I can step away to go to the front door, she holds my hands in hers, stopping me. Although she can't see me because of her vision loss, she tilts her chin up to look at me.

My grandma has glaucoma causing the loss of her vision due to her age and diabetes. It has been happening for two years now.

She sighs. "Where are you going? How about that college application? You haven't told me anything about it." Curiosity is laced in her voice.

I swallow and laugh nervously. If she could see me right now, she would probably figure out that I'm about to lie. "All set, Nana. Don't worry about it."

Guilt immediately washes over me because what I said was far from the truth. At the age of nineteen, I'm supposed to have already signed up for college. I probably should have been a sophomore this year. But it's not happening anytime soon.

I don't even know if I'm ever going to college. I can't afford it. We can't afford it.

But my Nana doesn't have to know. I don't want to see her crushed.

"I just have to go to the restaurant again for an extra shift this morning, but I'll be back for lunch," I squeeze her hands to assure her.

"You're still taking that part-time job?" Nana raises her brows. "I know that they pay well, but you work too hard. Now that you're going to college soon, you need more time to study--"

"Ssh." I kiss my grandma's cheek again, silencing her.

Every time she talks about my future, my heart sinks even lower because I know how much she dedicated her life to raising me.

"I know, Nana." My cheerful voice echoes, contrary to the turmoil in my heart. "I'm going to quit soon."

I mean what I said. I'm going to quit this job, but it's not for college. Instead of going to college, I'm going to find a new job, one that is far more rewarding because we need more money.

Nana, however, seems satisfied with my answer. She has no clue about what is going on.

"I'm going to be late. I have to go," I chirp, letting go of her hands and rushing toward the front door.

While I'm passing the living room, my eyes widen at the sight of the billing documents still scattering on the coffee table. Nana can't read it, but--

"What's that?"

I snap my head toward the source of the voice, and just as I was worried about, Archer emerges from the stairs.

Archer is my younger brother -- 14 years old -- and I love him dearly. He and Nana are the only family I still have.

I snatch the papers and abruptly shove them into my sling bag. "Just some college stuff." I grin sheepishly.

Archer yawns. "Did you get in?" he asks, still sounding sleepy.

"Absolutely," I pretend to brag, gripping the door handle.

I want to escape this conversation as soon as possible. My brother is too young to have this burden. He's been such a good boy, helping me and Nana without causing the troubles that most boys in his age would. Sometimes, he didn't spend some of the money I gave him -- which is way lesser than his friends would have -- just so we could buy more groceries. I'm really grateful to have him and Nana in my life.

"Which college--" Before Archer can finish his question about the college I'm going to, I push through the door.

The summer morning breeze greets me as soon as I step out of the house. I inhale the fresh air, letting out a sigh as I walk on the pavement.

I lied to Nana and Archer.

I'm not going to college. I can't. And now I'm not going to the restaurant to do my part-time job. Someone is going to interview me for a new one, and I hope that luck is on my side today.

I need more money. Urgently. I haven't even paid a quarter of Nana's hospital bills. The medical expenses for Nana's eye condition exceeded way more than what the insurance company could give us, but Nana doesn't know about that. She stops the treatment, but she has no idea that we were indebted.

Nana has suffered enough from losing her vision and learning that she can no longer take care of me and Archer. I don't have the heart to tell her that her disease caused more problems than she thought.

She has done so much for me and Archer since our parents were gone, and now it's my turn to make sacrifices for her. Postponing my college application for a year or two is nothing compared to what she did for us.

I swallow, watching as the middle-aged woman behind the desk in front of me studies me from head to toe.

I did my best to look presentable today. Although I'm wearing a pair of jeans and sneakers, I hope that the blazer makes me somehow look a little bit professional. I ran out of ideas on how to style my auburn hair, so I just tied it in a ponytail like usual.

The woman, who just introduced herself as Lauren, squints at me. "Interesting," she mumbles.

I raise my eyebrows, wondering what's on her mind. She shifts her attention to her computer, adjusts her glasses, and lets out a sigh which makes me think that she's been doing this interview for million years.

"I don't know why this person wants to hire you." She scrolls through the screen of her computer.

I don't think that she's a mean person for saying that. She seems genuinely, extremely curious.

My heart almost leaps in excitement because based on what she said, a potential client is interested to hire me.

She leans back against her chair and faces me again. "What made you apply to our home care services?"

I'm looking for money. Lots of them. My current part-time job doesn't help that much.

I feel like I almost blurted that out.

"Well, I've always been passionate about helping people." I smile.

She returns her eyes to her computer. "It states here that you applied for a job in companion care, homemaking care, hospice care support, live-in care, respite care..."

Correct. I literally applied for all of them. I'm that desperate for money.

"That's right," I say, a bit too enthusiastically. "I can take care of people with illness. I can also make sure that my client has someone to talk to. I can do the housekeeping, assist with laundry, prepare meals, or do other chores."

"Hm." Lauren's eyes are still glued to the screen. "But based on what I found here, you have no similar experience in your previous jobs."

My heart sinks at that, but I won't give up just yet. "I'm a very hardworking person and a fast learner."

While I'm trying to see what information on my resume she's reading, I catch a glimpse of my photo on the screen and instantly regret why I chose that picture.

I was smiling too much in that photo -- I thought that a cheerful picture might be good for this application, but then some clients might think that I just look plain stupid.

"It says here that you're used to taking care of your grandmother, though. And it's also stated here that she's blind?"

"Yes, she is," I say truthfully.

"Well, that might help." She hums, swirling her chair so that she faces me again. "Your client is also blind, Ms. Hayes."

Silence falls for a while.

My mouth drops open. "Are you saying that I got hired?" Disbelief is evident in my tone.

I don't think that the other fact is a problem because I'm used to taking care of my Nana. I don't mind looking after another blind person.

"Yes." Lauren nods.

I feel like rushing to her and hugging her tightly. Instead, I compose myself before I can do something embarrassing.

"Your profile, surprisingly, met the criteria for this client."

"Okay." My hands are getting sweaty from the excitement building up inside me. "How old is she? My client."

"He," Lauren corrects. "Your client is a man and a young one at that. He's only a year older than you."

I'm still trying to digest this information. "Does he expect personal care? Although I'm willing to take care of clients with disability, I remember putting some conditions on my application for that matter."

Uneasiness stirs inside me. If a guy around my age needs my help with personal tasks like bathing and dressing, I might not feel that comfortable and would end up disappointing him.

Lauren seems to notice my concern and shakes her head in assurance. "Don't worry. He is capable of doing all of that himself. In fact, he's even better than us in some areas."

My brows furrow in confusion.

"He's a blind martial artist," she adds.

"A what?"

"A martial artist. A fighter."

When she notices how dumbfounded I am, she chuckles. "Yes, it's remarkable, isn't it?"

I can only nod slowly. "It is."

My respect grows for this potential client. Even though he's blind, he has accomplished such ability. It's good for him.

But then, I squint at Lauren. "If that's the case, can you be more specific about what kind of help he needs from me? And what made him choose me out of the other applicants?"

Lauren sighs. "I was wondering too, especially about your last question. As for the details of your tasks, his assistant will be the one who will explain to you tomorrow. Should you be willing to take care of him, he will pay for your flight ticket from Chicago to Texas and pick you up at the airport."

My eyes instantly widen. There's one word in her sentence that makes me off guard. "Tomorrow?"

"Yes," Lauren says. "This client needs your help as soon as possible. He stated that it's urgent."

So many thoughts are running in my head. I can't let go of this opportunity. I'll do anything to help my family out of our money crisis. My Nana is blind, and Archer is too young to earn money.

I'm just not ready to tell them that I'm leaving them tomorrow. Will it be okay for Archer to take care of Nana alone while I'm gone?

"So, what do you think, Ms. Hayes?" Lauren is waiting for my response. "Do you think that you can take care of this client? We'll be discussing your payment first."

I take a deep breath, praying in my heart that I'm making the right decision and that everything will be okay.

5

CHAPTER 5

L AYLA

I drag my suitcase, stepping out of the arrival gate. My eyes travel around the airport, and once I spot the sign with my full name on it -- written in big, bold letters -- I totter toward it.

The man carrying it greets me, "Layla Hayes?"

I nod, flashing him a smile. "Yes. Are you Mr. Andy Wilson's assistant?"

I was told that my client, Andy, would send his assistant to pick me up. I'm just glad that I can find him because I have no idea where to go.

The man greeting me is wearing shades, so I can't really see his face. But he seems young, probably only a few years older than me. He's dressed in a black jacket, jeans and boots. He doesn't look formal.

"Welcome to Texas." He helps me carry my suitcase before I can decline his assistance, and I have no choice but to follow him toward the parking lot.

To say that I'm anxious would be an understatement.

I'd never thought that I would fly all the way here to work, but at the same time, I knew that I wouldn't be able to pass on this opportunity with how much the client would pay me.

Nana and Archer were no doubt shocked when I told them I had to be in Texas early to settle my living arrangements before starting college at Texas Tech University. I'd said that the apartment room I wanted to rent would be passed to someone else if I didn't come here today. They believed me.

When I step out of the building toward the parking lot, the sun is already setting. I wonder if I can sleep soundly tonight, knowing that I still have to adjust to the new unfamiliar place. I guess the tiredness will help -- I barely got enough sleep last night because of rushing to pack my things.

A black limo pulls up in front of us, causing me to raise my eyebrows in question. To my surprise, the man carrying my suitcase opens the door for me.

It turns out that Andy Wilson is super rich. I didn't expect that I would be picked up in a limo.

After the man puts my suitcase inside the trunk, he gets into the car after me instead of taking the seat beside the driver.

The driver, who's wearing a formal suit -- contrary to Andy's assistant -- starts driving, and that's when the assistant presses a button on the armrest that pulls the partition down. Maybe he wants to talk to me about something confidential, but that doesn't make me less alert because everything happening to me suddenly feels suspicious.

He takes off his sunglasses. "I'm sorry. I haven't introduced myself." He turns his head toward me, and now I can see his dark blue eyes which are in contrast with his blonde hair. A smile forms on his lips. "I'm Cole."

"Mr. Andy Wilson's assistant?" I question again.

Even though I know the answer, he didn't respond to that when I first saw him.

A sigh escapes from his mouth. "I am indeed your client's assistant, but I'm afraid that you'll be needing a lot more explanation."

My brows furrow. "What do you mean?"

He ignores my question, taking out his phone from his jacket pocket instead. While he's scrolling through his phone screen, I notice a tattoo on the inside of his wrist.

It's a tattoo of black wings, with red streaks. Although the tattoo is small, the wings have long, slotted feathers, each of which very detailed and well-crafted.

I'd never seen a tattoo so hypnotizing. It's scary that a tattoo can have such an impact on the person seeing it. The hair on the back of my neck suddenly stands, and I don't even know why. Cole has a dangerous aura I can't explain.

He seems to be reading a text from someone. "He just made the transfer of payment. You might want to check it."

With curiosity building up inside me, I take out my phone from my sling bag and notice a notification from my mobile banking. As soon as I open it, my eyes widen in shock.

The amount of money transferred to my bank account is beyond what I was told by the care agency. It's way too much, I have to recheck the number of zeros I'm seeing. With this money, not only I can pay all of Nana's debt for her medical bills but also the tuition fees for the most prestigious university in the country -- no, even in the world. I can even save it for Archer, for his future.

This is insane. My hand is shaking as I hold my phone.

"W-what?" I can't help but stutter.

It's not that I don't want the money -- this is the solution to all of my family's problems -- but there must be a mistake. A huge one.

"The payment was made in full amount instead of every month," the man beside me continues speaking casually like it's no big deal. "He paid in advance for your one-year contract."

I snap my head toward him. My eyes are wide while my chest is heaving up and down. "I'm sorry? There must be something wrong. I didn't apply for a job with this amount of payment."

"I know that this is a lot to take in, but unfortunately, Layla, he chose you."

"My client--"

"You won't be working for Andy Wilson," Cole interrupts. "You will be working for a very important person in our family, and when I say 'family', it means our organization. His name is Kellan Romero."

My heart almost stops because of this nonsense. Kellan Romero? I never heard of him.

"Well, I suggest you stop the car because this is definitely a huge misunderstanding," I say firmly even though my voice shakes a bit at the end of my sentence.

I can't help it. I'm in a car with strangers, and someone just paid me a ridiculous amount of money I still don't know what for.

"I will return the money," I say, ignoring how my heart sinks at that statement.

Just when I thought I could help Nana and Archer, my hope was crushed.

"And you will accept it because this is not the job I signed up for. There must have been a miscommunication with the agency." I swallow. "Unless this is some kind of kidnapping."

Cole's expression instantly turns serious the moment he hears the last word. "We are not kidnapping you, Layla. As I said, there's a lot to explain."

"Please do."

"This is indeed the job you were hired for," Cole says. "You signed up for live-in care, and I believe that the agency told you that your client lost his eyesight."

"Yes. I was informed about that."

"You will be working for Kellan," Cole says. "He's 20. Blind since he was 9. He needs help."

Something stings inside me after hearing that the person lost his eyesight when he was only a child. He was too young when he experienced such tragedy.

While I'm digesting this information, I realize that the same fact was uttered about this client I'm supposed to work for. The agency indeed told me that he was only a year older than me.

"But why was it stated that his name was Andy Wilson?" I ask. "Does the agency know about his real identity?"

Cole shakes his head. "Due to our working environment, we couldn't disclose it. Such information about Kellan Romero being blind might be portrayed as a weakness that could be used against us by our competitor. We prefer to keep things strictly confidential to outsiders. We have a team who always makes sure of that through the administrative process."

Cole's explanation only adds to my curiosity. If Kellan Romero and their organization are that important to the point that they couldn't even risk outsiders taking advantage of the classified information about his disability, why haven't I heard of him?

It's like I'm working for an under-protection family member of a military general with potential enemies, but the existence of that family itself is questionable.

Was it even legal what they did to the agency?

As though Cole can sense the burning question in my head, he adds, "You'll find out more about who we are and what we do when you arrive." He clears his throat, looking to the front. "Soon."

"Will I be involved in something illegal?" The question slips from my tongue.

Cole shakes his head again. "Nothing you will do can be categorized as illegal."

"I was told that I'll be helping a blind person, but the agency said that I would only get more details from you."

Cole nods. When his eyes find mine again, I notice how serious he is about this. I swallow the nervousness rising in my throat. Maybe I'm indeed going to do a very important job, and that's why they paid me really high. I just wish they weren't so secretive about this from the beginning because it makes me question a lot of things.

"First of all, the person who hired you was not Kellan himself," Cole says.

His sentence startles me.

"Then who?" I echo.

"Jaxon Romero, Kellan's older brother. He's the one who hired you."

I nod. "So he wants me to help his brother because he's blind. Did he use to have a helper before?"

Cole sighs, and I can hear a hint of desperation. "No. Surprisingly, you're going to be his first helper."

Cole closes his eyes and touches the crease of his eyebrows. He seems to be in deep thought all of sudden. "I guess Jaxon finally realized that Kellan needed someone, especially while he was away."

"Away?"

"Jaxon is in Italy." Cole opens his eyes again. A look of determination crosses his expression. "He's been there for years. I was assigned to work with him, which is why I have to go back there as soon as possible."

I'm about to ask more questions when he continues speaking, facing me again. "Look, you have two tasks." Cole is studying me, as though he's trying to see if I'm the right person for it. "First, while you're living in the house, you have to assist Kellan at all times. And second, if he goes out, you have to accompany him. He can't go out without you. He rarely does, anyway, so you may think less about the second one. Kellan prefers to spend most of his time in the house, no matter how suffocated he feels."

"Can you tell me more about him?" Just as I say those words, I see sadness glinting in Cole's eyes.

"Kellan has a painful past, and I don't think that he has recovered from that," Cole says. "He lost his eyesight in a car crash, in which his parents and little sister died. He was the only survivor in that accident, and he was still a little boy at that time."

My hand shoots to my mouth. I can't imagine what Kellan went through.

It was tragic.

I don't know how a little boy could recover from that traumatic incident, mentally. One would never recover from it.

Cole's jaw tightens, as though he's angry that such fate happened and that there's nothing we can do about it. "Kellan accepted that fate, but he can't let go of his grudge. Martial arts help him let out his anger, but still, it's not enough."

My stomach churns with every word coming out of Cole's mouth. I'm starting to doubt if I'm good enough for this job.

"Unfortunately, Jaxon can't look out for him all the time, especially now that most of us have to finish our task in Italy," Cole says with slight guilt in his voice. "Kellan needs someone to take care of him."

I knew that I had to be prepared to give mental support to a person with a disability when I accepted the job, but I didn't expect this kind of story.

"But why me?" My voice is a whisper, filled with uncertainty. "There are many other applicants who are professionals and might be more qualified to be his helper. Why did you entrust him to me?"

I'm just a girl with no experience who is used to taking care of my blind grandmother. I'm nobody compared to professional caregivers.

"I'm not sure. As I said, Jaxon chose you out of the other applicants." Cole leans back against the seat. "Anyway, he told me that most of them are way older, while he wanted someone around the same age as Kellan to be his friend."

I go silent, shifting my gaze toward the window as I allow my thoughts to wander around the possibility of what may happen.

The longer the journey continues, the more I feel nervous. I've always been optimistic, but something about the atmosphere around me -- this car, the deserted street around me, and Cole -- makes me strangely uncomfortable like there's something more of it.

"I hope that you're not changing your mind after hearing my explanation. I'm afraid that it's too late to do that now," Cole's voice echoes beside me.

My heart starts to beat rapidly inside my chest. The rest of the ride is too silent, and there are times I feel Cole's eyes on me like he's trying to figure out what kind of person I really am.

The air inside the car feels colder although nobody changes the temperature, and I'm starting to wonder if I'm having either a hallucination or panic attack. Even the street outside seems odd and the night turns darker.

We're passing an area where the houses around us are too big with yards that seem to never end -- probably the owners don't even know their neighbors. The longer we continue our journey, there are fewer houses we pass.

Until there is none.

Not only the houses are missing but also the street lamps.

On the other side of the window, it's pitch black. I can't see anything. If it's not for the car headlights illuminating the road in front of us, I'm sure that the driver won't even make it and we will be stuck in this darkness.

My hands are sweaty as I hold them on my lap. My brain and my body are telling me to change my mind. My instinct is warning me that something is wrong with this job and that I shouldn't be here.

But my heart -- even though it's racing right now -- can't help but think about the young man staying inside this house I will step into.

Lonely.

Blind.

The darkness, just like the one surrounding us now, is the only thing he sees every time he opens his eyes. He doesn't even have any single light to guide him like what we have now to help us through this road.

I look up at the sky through the car window, and even though a sense of comfort washes over me when I find the moon shining through the darkness of the night for all kinds of creatures, my heart breaks because he doesn't even have it, not even just as dimmed as the moon when it's hidden by the clouds.

I know the pain of losing both parents. Even though the wound might heal, we're never going to stop missing them.

Kellan had it worse because it happened so suddenly. They were taken in a blink of an eye.

I know how devastated Nana was when she lost her sight. It was so, so hard for me and Archer to remind her that it wasn't the end when her world crumbled. Those times were the hardest for our family.

And Kellan also went through all of that, worse than what Archer, Nana, and I did.

My heart is telling me to stay. Maybe Kellan and I can indeed be friends. I would be glad to help him have at least one thing -- a friend. Just like his brother wants me to be for him.

The car slows down, making a turn. When I look out the window again, my breath catches in my throat.

There before my eyes is a gate so tall. It reminds me of the gate attached to a fortress to block enemies during war.

The car stops, and Cole rolls down the window beside him. He doesn't even have to turn his head to face the guard outside. One second is all needed for the guard to bark some commands urgently, causing the gate to open. Behind it stands a building that sucks out the air in my lungs.

It's definitely not a house.

All I can see is a mansion, the biggest one I've ever seen. Lights, so many of them, dimmed through the windows. And cars parked around the driveway. A dozen of them.

6

CHAPTER 6

L AYLA

The car stops in the driveway. Cole steps out and opens the door for me while the driver gets my suitcase from the trunk.

I'm sure that Cole can see how nervous I am -- I can't even move my legs to step out of this car. He just nods, giving me a look of assurance.

After taking a deep breath, I brace myself to get out. There's no way that I'm going to back down from this job now.

I look up at the massive building before me, the three-story Italian Renaissance-style mansion. It looks even more intimidating now that I'm seeing it up close.

I follow Cole, walking up behind him. A guy stands between us and the huge double doors, preventing us from entering. He looks like a security guard but doesn't dress like it -- more like a cruel gangster I'd rather see in a movie than face in reality. My legs automatically stop as I see the shotgun he's holding. A small scream almost escapes from my throat as the guy pushes Cole's chest with the tip of the shotgun.

"Identity," the guy speaks with authority, studying Cole from head to toe. Even though we passed the security at the gate, this guy wouldn't just let us in.

Cole chuckles lightly, but the voice that comes out of his mouth is so cold, it makes the hair on the back of my neck stand. "You must be new, huh?"

The guy frowns at Cole's question. Cole raises his hands, and the guy's eyes widen in shock as soon as he sees the tattoo crafted on Cole's right wrist. He doesn't just lower his gun -- he literally drops it, causing it to clatter on the ground.

What startles me even more is that the guy drops to his knees and quickly apologizes. When he does that, I notice a small tattoo of black wings on the back of his neck. It's the same tattoo as Cole's, but while Cole has red streaks on the feathers, this guy has none. It's just a pair of black wings.

Another guard rushes to carry my suitcase. I can only watch helplessly when he inspects my belongings in front of the door. He rummages through my garments like I would have brought an actual bomb with me.

"She's a recruit," Cole tells the guy inspecting my suitcase, making him nod.

I turn my back to them and wrap my arms around my waist. Strangely, the air feels too cold for a summer night, sending chills through my body. God, this place is making me crazy even though I haven't even started my job.

When I turn around, Cole is reading a text from his phone. A frown touches his lips before he shoves his phone back into his pants pocket.

"I gotta go," he says to me. "My flight to Italy was rescheduled. I have to fly there earlier than I thought."

I don't know what to say to him. The circumstances make it difficult to say no, but I also find it impossible to say that I'm going to like this job.

Cole seems to notice my fear and doubt. He places his palm on my shoulder to comfort me. "I know that you may not find this job easy, but please stay close to Kellan. The two of you need each other here. It's what keeps you both safe if something bad happens."

Before I can ask him what that means, Cole strides toward the car, and in a matter of seconds, he's gone. I can only watch with my mouth agape as the car leaves the property through the gate.

"Hey, new girl."

The harsh tone startles me, causing me to abruptly turn around. The guy who just finished checking my suitcase motions with his finger to come closer to him.

I swallow. Every step I'm taking to erase the distance between us feels like forever. I'm not used to people carrying guns, especially when they're not dressed in security uniforms -- and when they can point the guns at me without hesitation.

"Your phone." He almost rolls his eyes, as though I'm stupid.

And yes, maybe I am. I don't understand him at all. I can only gawk at him with a blank expression.

"My phone?"

He scoffs. "Yes, your damn phone."

Instinctly, I grip the small sling bag I'm wearing, in which I have my phone. A sense of protectiveness hits me.

Why would he ask for my phone? What is he going to do with it?

Without warning, he storms in my direction. "Do you prefer me inspecting your body? Or do you want to hand it yourself?"

I step back in fear. The need to protect myself screams at me, so I take out my phone. My hand is shaking when I give it to him.

He snatches my phone, flips it around, and cracks open the casing to take out the battery. Then he examines my phone thoroughly, as though there would be a tracker attached to it.

"Give it back." It's surprising that I still dare to order him.

Apparently, it's a bad idea. The other guy -- who bowed to Cole earlier -- pushes my back with his gun, causing my body to jerk forward. My heart almost stops.

"Just get inside and stop bitching around." He pushes the barrel against my back again to make me walk faster. Now that Cole is out of sight, he doesn't think twice about treating me harshly. "Don't even think about breaking the rules."

What is he talking about? Is there some kind of rules here I have to follow?

How would I contact Archer and Nana if I don't have my phone with me?

"But, my phone--" I don't even have time to finish my complaint because the guy pushes me through the door and shuts it.

What's happening inside the mansion shocks me. I'm petrified like a statue.

Here, it's totally different from the outside.

Here, it's loud and filled with so many people -- no wonder they have a dozen cars out there.

I didn't expect that I would be walking into a party -- a freaking party where people are drinking and dancing, lost in their own world. Deep thumping music rings in my ears while my eyes are scanning around the place.

I'm greeted with a huge area with a high ceiling that makes me feel like I just stepped into a ballroom, but it's nothing like that in a fairytale. The interiors and furniture are all dark, I feel like I was just shoved into an ancient castle.

Two spiral staircases stand on each side of the hall, and when I look up, it only confirms my thought of how majestic this place is. There are corridors on the second floor, leading to more rooms and more parts of the house.

When my gaze darts back to where I'm standing, all I can see are people. And more people. They're talking. Laughing. Making out. Kissing. Bodies are moving in sync with the music beat.

There's only one thing surfacing in my head: I don't belong here. What the hell am I doing in this place?

I hear a boisterous laugh somewhere in the distance, and then someone bumps me in the shoulder quite hard.

"Sorry," the person says to me.

As I turn, I see a pretty girl with tanned skin and black eyes. I'm still overwhelmed by the surroundings, so I can only stare at her blankly instead of responding to her apology.

She squints at me, a strand of her curly hair falling over her face as she stands tipsily.

A guy with light brown hair and pale skin stands next to her, draping his arm around her shoulder. He stares at me curiously. "I haven't seen you around."

Uneasiness stirs inside me. "Yeah, I'm kinda new."

The girl's brows furrow. "Who brought you here?"

I swallow. "A guy named Cole."

She looks like she's trying to digest what I said, and then her eyes widen in shock. "You're kidding me. Cole Madden?"

I don't know what she meant by that, but it seems that Cole is quite famous here -- I remember that the guy guarding the door instantly dropped to his knees after noticing the tattoo on Cole's wrist.

"Actually, I don't know his last name," I mumble.

The girl laughs. "There's only one Cole in this family, and there's no way that he just recruited you."

I'm about to tell her that I was hired by Jaxon Romero to take care of his blind brother, but before I can open my mouth, the guy chirps in, "Technically, he could," he says to her in an amused tone. "He's a Knight."

The girl rolls her eyes. "Of course. What I'm saying is that he wouldn't recruit just anybody. Cole wouldn't." She studies me from head to toe, almost snickering. "And she doesn't look like she can fight. Pretty sure that she's not the kind of newbie Jaxon would approve."

I'm officially lost. I don't know what they were talking about and what kind of nonsense this is all about.

"You mean, Jaxon Romero?" I press.

The girl stares at me in disbelief. "Now you're talking as if you don't even know our king." Suddenly, a look of pity crosses her expression. "Are you here because someone bullied you in Truth or Dare? Or are you here for a bet? This kind of thing never gets old." She sighs, shaking her head.

"Seems like the first one," the guy speaks like he's trying to hold back laughter, tossing me the same look of pity.

I really want to leave this place because of the way they make me feel even more uncomfortable, but a part of me wants to know what they're trying to say.

"I'm Brea, by the way. And this is my boyfriend, Gio." She extends her arm for a handshake while Gio bursts out laughing, as though she just made up their names.

I reluctantly accept the handshake.

"You are...?" She raises her brow in question.

"Layla," I say.

Brea grabs my arm and drags me further into the house until we stand under the staircase, away from people dancing and talking even though the music and noises are still pretty loud in my ears.

"Well, Layla." Brea looks at me intently, lowering her voice. "Normally, we don't do this. One would expect to be buried six feet under if they dared step into this place. But..." Her eyes glint with mischief. "Consider this as our generosity. We won't tell anyone that you sneaked in."

"You're fucking crazy," Gio blurts out to her, but he can't hide the adoration on his face when he stares at his girlfriend. Her daring personality may be the reason why he likes her.

"Come on, I was once bullied too," she purrs, leaning into him as she playfully touches his chest. "Besides, Truth or Dare is always my thing." She returns her attention to me and smiles. "So...Layla."

She sighs while I involuntarily hold my breath, preparing for what she's about to say. The longer I stay in this place, the more anxious I become because of the unexpected things I find.

"You and your friends might think that using our leaders' names -- Cole, or even Jaxon -- would save you and make it less suspicious.

But..." She tsks. "You're fucking wrong. If you don't understand how things work here, you'll be in big trouble."

7

CHAPTER 7

L AYLA

Brea corrects, "No, it won't be just trouble. It will cost your life. The people here won't hesitate to put a bullet in your head, and it will be the most generous way to end your life here besides the other things we can do to you."

My mouth drops open. I don't want to believe her, but the things I saw and experienced today -- especially my conversation with Cole and what happened with the guards outside -- make me think that she's not lying.

"Tell me, how much will your friends pay you for getting out of here alive?" Her face draws closer, causing me to be cornered against the wall under the stairs. "How much are they willing to pay for you to sneak into the home of the Black Wings?"

I almost freeze like a statue. What did she just say? The Black Wings?

Still hearing nothing from me, she squints.

I can only say the truth. "I'm not here because of a bet, or a dare." She rolls her eyes.

"Are you saying that you are one of us?" Gio asks, but his tone doesn't sound genuine. It sounds like he's testing me.

"I don't know if being hired by your leader will make me one," I say. "Honestly, I don't care about that. I just want to see Kel--"

"Show me your tattoo," Brea interrupts.

I stare at her cluelessly. "My what?"

"Your tattoo," Gio repeats, sounding annoyed. "Your identity. It will show that you are indeed one of us. Here, the tattoo is proof that you're a part of Black Wings."

Of course, I don't have that. I never plan to be a part of the Black Wings or whatever gang it is.

"Like this." Brea shows me a tattoo on her upper arm. It's a pair of black wings, but unlike Cole's tattoo which has red streaks on the feathers, this one has none. "Show me yours."

I'm at a loss for words. How can I show her if I don't even have a tattoo?

When she finally gets the idea, she mutters, "You can't be serious. You couldn't just sneak here without even preparing your tattoo."

Gio snorts. "Even if she did, we would notice that it's fake, so it doesn't matter."

Brea nods, agreeing with her boyfriend. "Right. Every Black Wings tattoo is specially made by our artists, with special inks. Only two people in this world can make our tattoos. It's sickening how some people still think that they can fake it. At least, you're not one of them."

Gio chuckles. "Your lies have been caught, Layla."

Their accusation makes me feel offended. "I'm not lying. I didn't say that I was one of you. I'm not interested in joining your gang, the Black Wings, or whatever it is. I'm here because I was hired by Jaxon Romero. Cole brought me here--"

"Whoa whoa whoa." Brea raises her hands, staring at me in utter disbelief. "You're going too far right there."

"I don't have time to deal with people who don't even want to believe me," I say firmly. "Now, if you'll excuse me--"

"Wait." Gio grabs my arm before I can escape. Now, he looks slightly furious. "What you were trying to say didn't make fucking sense. We were about to let you slip without harm, but now you're being feisty and thinking about leaving just like that?" The threat in his voice makes me shudder.

"Aw, easy, babe. You're scaring her," Brea whispers to him, giving him a sweet smile. "She's doing her best to survive. I like that spirit in her. Who knows? We might convince Fenrir to make her one of us. She might be useful." She turns her head toward me. "Now, where were we? Ah, you said that you were hired by Jaxon."

The three of us turn silent. I'm waiting for her to say more, trying to block the noises from the party.

I hate parties.

But then, Brea laughs boisterously. Gio chuckles again, shaking his head. "You can do better, little liar."

"I'm not lying," I say, raising my tone.

"That's impossible," Brea says like it's the most obvious thing in the world. "Jaxon couldn't have hired you. If he had, you would have had your Black Wings tattoo with red streaks on it. There are only three people in this fucking world who have it. So far, you have none." She pauses, raising her eyebrows. "Unless you can show me."

"Dream on." Gio smirks. "That's why little liars like you never survive this place. They always come here with zero clues about how things work here."

"I'm a caregiver--"

"Your lies have been exposed, Layla." Brea corners me again, and my back is pushed against the wall. "Did you actually think that it would make sense to create that kind of story so that you could step into this place?" She then urges her boyfriend, "Show her yours, babe."

Gio flips his left arm, showing me a tattoo of black wings on the inside of his upper arm.

"This is mine," he says. "My identity. You can't be here without it. The punishment is death. You can't fake it either. Same punishment -- death. I wonder how the fuck you could pass the guards outside. I'll make a note to tell Fenrir about that. The guys have been pretty lazy nowadays."

I don't have any idea about this man named Fenrir. It seems like he's one of their leaders.

Now that I'm staring closely at Gio's tattoo, it indeed has the same effect as the one I saw on Cole's wrist. It's hypnotizing. The tattoo is very detailed and well-crafted, it makes me feel like I'm seeing the real thing -- a pair of black wings.

Panic starts to build up inside me. Cole didn't tell me anything about the tattoo. He only warned me to stay close to Kellan so that everything would be alright.

What am I supposed to do?

"The black wings tattoo is the identity for all the regular members," Brea says matter-of-factly. "You just stepped into our base. Not only you didn't have your identity, but you were trying to fool us with some ridiculous made-up story."

I'm about to open my mouth again, but Brea drags me along the hidden wall under the staircase before I can utter another word.

When she halts, my eyes land on the four polaroid photos attached to the wall.

"Fortunately, we have the photos of our leaders down here so you can have a better idea about how fucked up your lies were," she says.

"Fangirls," Gio retorts while Brea rolls her eyes at him.

The first photo is of Cole in a black leather jacket, smoking a cigarette. He's not looking at the camera. It's a candid picture. He looks good, just as he does in real life, but the monochrome photo doesn't do any justice to his captivating blue eyes.

"That's Cole, and I doubt you've ever met him. He's in Italy fighting our enemies," Brea says. "He's one of the Knights, which means that he has a black wings tattoo with red streaks. Kings choose Knights, and Knights choose regular members. If you were recruited by a Knight, you would have a regular black wings tattoo like what I have. Unfortunately, Cole never recruits. He couldn't have hired you."

My fist curls into a fist. "I never said he did." I'm itching to tell her that I did meet this man, but she'll never believe me anyway.

"But you did say that he brought you here. That's impossible too," she hums. "Now the second picture. His name is Levi. One of the Knights as well. He's our King's most trusted right-hand man, other than Cole, of course."

My gaze darts on the second photo. The man is sitting on his motorcycle, not looking at the camera. Again, another candid photo. He has dark hair, but I can't see his eyes clearly because he's looking at his phone. Nothing can hide how attractive he is, though.

"Levi rarely talks. He doesn't do people," Brea blabbers. "The only things he's interested in are weapons and blood. He's not even interested in women, or men, if you know what I mean. He's a killing machine. If you told us that Levi ever talked to you, we would know in an instant that you were lying."

That's enough for me to learn how scary this guy is. "I don't know him." I shrug, telling the truth.

We move to the third photo, which shows a man dressed in all black walking from a limo. Although it's just a piece of photo, the way the man carries himself sends shivers down my spine. His expression can make any people cower. His aura speaks of danger.

"That's Jaxon," Brea says with pride and excitement. "He's our King, the heir of the Romero family who creates this place. His father was the founder of Black Wings."

I look closer, studying Jaxon's face.

"Rumors spread," Brea says. "People might have heard his name, but they never know his face. Only the members of Black Wings have seen him in person, and just a few of them. Personally, I haven't even met him."

"Now you know why we wouldn't believe you," Gio adds. "There's no way that Jaxon suddenly recruited a girl like you. He only hired people like Cole and Levi."

"More like his personal bodyguards." Brea chuckles and points at me. "Are we clear?"

I want to counter her argument, but curiosity makes me pop a question instead. "How old is Jaxon?"

"24," Brea says. "Same age as Cole. Levi is younger. He's 20, the same age as Kellan, Jaxon's brother. He's next."

My heart thumps. Kellan. I want to know more about this person I'm going to take care of.

I haven't met him, but now I can finally see his face in the picture.

My eyes land on the last picture attached to the wall, and my breath catches in my throat. The photo shows a man standing inside a boxing ring. He's shirtless, full of sweat and panting. I can see his toned abs and how well-built he is, but that's not the only thing catching my attention.

His expression is something that one wouldn't miss. He looks angry. Like, really angry. He's seething.

"What a beautiful sight, huh?" Brea points out, and I know from her voice that she can't help the smile on her face. "This candid picture is a masterpiece. Some girls get off imagining that."

I wish she could keep that information to herself.

"Kellan is our king too, but sadly, he's blind," Gio says, making me swallow.

I've heard about the tragedy that made Kellan lose his eyesight. My heart hurts for the little boy, who obviously has grown up. He's not a little boy anymore, but I can still see the pain in his eyes through this picture.

"Kellan, just like Jaxon, has a black wings tattoo with silver streaks," Gio says. "That kind of tattoo belongs to the heirs of Romero, and they are Kings here."

My pulse quickens. Their explanation makes me realize even more how powerful my client is. Doubts begin to cloud my mind again, I'm not sure that I can handle this job. Kellan has already looked intimidating in my eyes even though I only saw his photo.

Something is not fitting, though. "You said that regular members are hired by Knights, and Knights are hired by the Kings," I say. "So who hired you?"

It's either Cole or Levi. But based on their explanation about those two people, it's highly unlikely.

"Fenrir," Brea says. "He's the other Knight. Even though he's not our King, he's no less than God here. Jaxon, Cole, and Levi have been in Italy for years, while Fenrir runs things here. Most of us were recruited by him."

"You wouldn't want to mess with Fenrir," Gio adds. "Even Jaxon and Kellan look up to him. He used to be their father's right-hand man."

After a moment of silence, Gio speaks again, "This is the kind of information you would take to the grave. Now that you've heard about our leaders, there's no way that you will go back to wherever it is you belong."

I turn toward Brea, who gives me a knowing smile.

"I'm sorry." She shrugs. "I wasn't planning to spill you something that would cost your life, but your lies were terrible. Might as well shove the truth with all the consequences, right?"

Gio steps toward me, and his voice is filled with thrill and excitement when he says, "Now, the question is..." he pauses, eyeing me with interest. "What should we do with an intruder like you?"

I brace myself, straightening up. "Just bring me to Kel--"

Before I can finish my sentence, a loud voice echoes in the air.

"Boxing ring! Now!"

Then it all happens so fast. Someone shouts from upstairs. The music abruptly stops. Whispers of excitement fill the air. Footsteps pound on the ground. People are suddenly rushing in the same direction.

I can only watch what's happening around me in shock.

Now what?

I snap my head around, and surprisingly, Brea and Gio are already gone to follow the crowd.

While I'm trying to make my way out through the people, a guy bumps into me. I can't help but ask, "What's happening?"

"Kellan is fighting, and you don't want to miss it." He glances back at me just for a second before rushing to the basement where everyone is heading.

8

CHAPTER 8

LAYLA

I can't help but bring my legs toward the basement. I push myself through the crowd, following the people who are way too excited to see what's about to happen.

When I finally arrive, I manage to secure a nice spot, just a few steps away from the ring -- thanks to my petite figure slipping easily between these bodies of strangers.

The moment my eyes are glued to the person standing on the ring, my heart skips a beat.

There, standing tall in the middle of it, is Kellan Romero. His chest heaves up and down, as though he just finished running even though the fight hasn't even begun.

He looks more masculine than the one I saw just now in the picture. His defined muscles look even more intimidating but also beautiful like a piece of art -- does that even make sense?

He's taller than I expected, so tall -- the picture doesn't do him any justice. His hair is dark and messy, almost close to jet black. And his eyes... My God, his eyes... they're the most captivating eyes I've ever seen. They are grey -- misty and mysterious and hold so much more.

He's angry -- I can see it from his expression -- but there's also something else. Sadness? Grief? Pain?

He's very expressive, I almost can feel his emotions myself. Am I the only one who notice it? I don't know, but I can't take my eyes off him.

When Kellan turns the other way, I see the massive black wings tattooed all over his shoulders and back. The tattoo is nothing compared to the other black wings tattoo I saw today. His is enormous, magnificent. It even looks like he has actual wings, which makes him look like an angel -- not like the stereotype angel, but more like a dark angel. A dark, lethal angel.

I don't know how long I've been staring at him, until our eyes suddenly meet. He frowns in my direction, and my heart thumps. It's impossible that he notices me -- he's blind. But I swear, he does, somehow.

Those beautiful grey eyes can't see me -- he doesn't meet my gaze-- but he looks in my direction with such curiosity, that I wonder if my intense gaze has been affecting him.

His opponent steps onto the ring, catching his attention. The crowd cheers, but I notice some people shaking their heads, as though they're underestimating what's about to happen. Some of them even have pity written on their faces like they expect one of the fighters to be beaten into a pulp.

It seems that Kellan's opponent is around the same age. His body is also well built with broad shoulders, but he doesn't look as intimidating as Kellan. His nostrils flare while Kellan's chest heaves up. Kellan takes a deep breath, a sign that he's trying to calm his temper before the fight begins.

"I don't understand why they never learn from their mistakes," a girl watching beside me is talking to her friend. "How are they supposed to complete Fenrir's task if they can't even defeat a blind man?"

Her friend laughs. "I don't care. We get to enjoy their practice session. We're lucky Kellan is the trainer for our fighters, and it seems that he always enjoys giving them a hard time."

When another guy in the ring gives the sign to start the fight with his hand, my heart starts to race. Kellan is blind -- I don't know how he's going to win this fight.

The other guy attacks first, and I almost gasp as Kellan dodges his punch. When he tries to land a kick, Kellan blocks it, whirls to lift his opponent's body, and then throws him harshly onto the ground.

Kellan's opponent groans in pain as the back of his head smacks the hard cement. I wince. I'm not used to violence, and a part of me wants to leave immediately. Yet, my feet feel like being nailed onto the ground. I'm being hypnotized by the sight before me -- Kellan, especially.

How could a blind person move so fast and so easily? It's almost as if he can feel his opponent's movement before the guy launches the next attack.

Watching Kellan fighting is like watching a beautiful piece of art slowly being unleashed before my eyes. He moves so quickly, and gracefully, like he was the wind and that nothing could stop him.

Ironically, Kellan also looks more composed when he fights. He's now less angry and a lot calmer than he was before the fight, as though he finally gains control.

I read somewhere that losing one of your senses might strengthen the other senses, and I think it happens to Kellan. He lost his eyesight, but his ability to feel and hear, as well as his reflexes, are better than normal people.

Kellan lands a powerful kick on his opponent's ribs, tossing him against the rope across the ring. A loud 'Ouch' echoes from the crowd. The poor guy snaps his head toward Kellan. He glares at the blind martial artist, spitting blood from his mouth.

Anyone can see how much the guy wants to defeat Kellan, but just as he storms again at Kellan, Kellan ducks and kicks him on the leg, making him fall. Before he can even get up, Kellan aims another kick. The guy freezes as Kellan's foot stops mere inches from the pulse on his neck. It's a dead end for him. Kellan wins.

"If this happened in your mission, you would be fucking dead," Kellan's voice echoes. He then turns his head toward the other side of the ring and hisses, "Next fighters better not call me before you win a fight against him."

The crowd roars at the victory of their king, and only then do I realize that I've been panting. This is crazy. I never thought that watching a real fight would make my heart beat so rapidly.

Kellan steps down from the ring. While he's making his way through the people who automatically step aside to let him walk, I rush toward him.

"Wait." My voice is muffled as the crowd roars again to welcome another fighter stepping onto the stage to challenge the guy who just got beaten by Kellan.

"Kellan," I shout, but my effort is to no avail because the voices around me are too loud.

Panic begins to consume me when I see him about to disappear into the crowd. He's the only one who will understand why I'm here, and I'm supposed to assist him at all times inside this house, just as Cole told me to.

I quicken my pace, and the moment I see his back, I impulsively stretch my arm to reach him. I'm about to touch him when he suddenly whirls around. He snaps my hand off, pushing me backward and making me stumble until I fall to the ground.

I wince in pain, looking up to see him, only to find him glaring in my direction. His jaw tightens, as though his body is sending him signals that I'm a threat.

Kellan is blind, but his reflexes are so damn good, resulting from his primal need to protect himself.

People abruptly stop what they are doing to watch us. I'm too shaken to stand up. They are staring down at me and forming a circle around me and Kellan. I might be the only one here who dared touch their King -- that fact is enough to divert their attention from the boxing ring, as though what's happening here is much more interesting.

Kellan is still seething in front of me. I have to explain.

Slowly, I stand on my feet. "Sorry that I startled you."

He frowns. His anger is still very much visible, but I can see a bit of curiosity too from his face.

I swallow. "This might not be the best way to introduce myself." I scan the crowd around us, who seem to grow more quiet the more seconds pass. Then I return my gaze to Kellan. "Do you mind if we talk somewhere else?"

Privately, I beg in my heart. Being the center of attention like this is too much for me.

"Speak now. Here," Kellan says in a commanding tone, leaving me no room to argue.

I have no obligation to obey that kind of command, but I have a feeling that going against him now would lead to more trouble.

I straighten my spine, taking a deep breath. "I'm Layla, your new caregiver. Your brother, Jaxon, hired me to take care of you and assist you."

Jaxon must have informed him about me, so he should be expecting me, shouldn't he?

But then, Kellan looks slightly taken aback. It's not a good sight, especially since I notice the irritated look on his expression. I hear some people trying to muffle their laughter while the others scoff.

My brows furrow in confusion as I wait for Kellan's response. He closes his eyes and shakes his head in disbelief. When those grey eyes return to me, I see the same fury that greeted me a while ago.

"Do you think that I need a fucking caregiver?" he bites out, making my heart sink. "Do you actually think that I do?"

No one makes any sound, anticipating what he'll say next. I don't even know if the fight inside the boxing ring is still happening -- it probably isn't -- because the silence that follows after he speaks is excruciating.

"Get lost." With that said unbearably coldly, Kellan turns around and leaves.

9

Chapter 9

KELLAN

Fucking ridiculous.

I never thought that such a liar existed among Black Wings members. How the hell did Fenrir recruit the newcomers?

I storm into my room with my fists clenched tightly on my sides. My chest rises and falls because of my anger.

The fight inside the boxing ring earlier might have calmed me down, but that girl just made me even angrier. She even mentioned Jaxon, and that story she made up was insane.

There's no way that Jaxon would hire a caregiver for me.

Layla, her name. Who does she think she is?

Fucking poser.

The sound of my phone ringing on my bed catches my attention, and I instantly scoff because I know who the caller is from the ringtone.

About time, Jaxon is calling me. I usually don't answer his call, but maybe I should now.

I grab my phone, feeling that I might break it because of how hard I'm gripping it. This is fucking irritating.

The second I answer Jaxon's call, his voice echoes in my ear. "Finally." He lets out a long sigh. "About damn time you pick up my call."

I listen closely to any other sound from the other side of the line and only hear faintly Levi ordering food to someone.

No gunshot sound. I feel slightly relieved because no matter how much I hate what Jaxon is doing over there in Italy with the guys, he's not in danger right now.

I hear a light chuckle. "Wait, have you already met her?" Amusement is now laced in his voice.

I clench my jaw, feeling like I'm going to explode. If it's actually true about the girl, I'll be fucking mad at him.

"No wonder you picked up my call." Although his tone is joking, I can feel his disappointment. "I had to drag some girl into this for you to pick up your brother's call, huh?" he throws me a rhetorical question, which annoys me even more.

"I'll hang up--"

"Wait," Jaxon immediately says, and I hear slight anger in his voice. "Jesus Christ. Kellan, calm the fuck down."

"You know damn well why I never want to pick up your call," I say coldly. "If you want to hear my voice that badly, you can drag your ass back here."

Jaxon lets out a heavy sigh. "Quit being a brat. You know perfectly well why I have to be in Italy and why you can't be here."

I scoff. "Yeah? Because I'm fucking blind--"

"Kellan," Jaxon says to me in a warning tone. "You know why you can't be in Italy, and we're not doing this anymore."

I almost roll my eyes.

Yeah. Because it's fucking dangerous there, and you're not letting me there because you don't want me to die. You're leaving me here with no choice other than to accept that you could die anytime.

"Why did you even hire her?" I ask, not even trying to hide my irritation.

"Because you need her," Jaxon says.

Silence falls.

"What the hell does that mean?" I holler.

Jaxon sighs. "Listen, you're always angry," he pauses, as though he needs a few seconds to compose himself. "I know that you don't think you need a caregiver, but I do think that you need one."

Before I can even interrupt him, he continues, "It's not that I think you are incapable, but I need someone to look after you while I'm gone." His voice holds vulnerability, and for a second, I think that my brother is going to break.

I hate this. I fucking hate a situation in which I can't do anything to make it better.

"I have looked through some care agencies," Jaxon says. "I just want you to have a friend. Layla is around the same age as you, a bit younger, as I remember. She has a family member who is also blind, so she's used to taking care of someone blind who is close to her. I know for a fact that she needs money, and I think she's not the kind of girl that will cost you trouble."

If Jaxon didn't sound that serious right now, I would laugh out loud because of how ridiculous it was.

I just can't imagine my brother, Jaxon Romero, digging into a care agency and trying to find a girl to take care of me.

"Seriously?" I almost shout in frustration. "A girl?"

Jaxon lets out a small chuckle. "What?" I can imagine him raising an eyebrow. "Would you prefer me to hire a dude to take care of you?" His sense of humor might kill me someday. "Are you still mad that I brought Cole and Levi here with me?"

My nostrils flare. Now, he's reminding me that it wouldn't only be him who could get his head shot there but also my best friends. I don't like people, but strangely, Cole and Levi have no problem hanging around me.

"Cole will be ecstatic to hear that you miss him," he says in amusement, "but Levi...you know him. He will shoot you if you say that you miss him." Jaxon tsks. "He's one cold-hearted man." It's clear from Jaxon's voice that he's trying to muffle his laughter.

"You're enjoying this, huh?" I say sarcastically.

"Come on." I can imagine him grinning smugly. "Let's look at the bright side of this. I just hired her, and you already picked up my call. Judging from my experiences, it's one in a million chance."

My blood is boiling. "Rather than waiting for me to pick up your call, you could just drag your ass back here."

Jaxon sighs. I know that I'm being childish again, but I just don't want to hear that my brother died on a mission. He's the only family I still have.

I distinctly hear Levi reminding him to be quick from the other side of the line, and my heart sinks, knowing that he's about to be in danger again.

"I have to go," Jaxon says, already lowering his voice down because of whatever happening there. "You may have a hard time warming up to her in the beginning, but give her a chance."

I grip the phone in my hand tightly, trying to hold my anger down and knowing that I can't escape this. If there's one thing that I will regret later, it's disappointing my brother.

I sense that he will hang up, so I quickly say, "Wait. Before you go, I need you to clarify it one more time."

Jaxon doesn't say anything. All I can hear is the sound of a car door slamming shut and tires screeching, but I know that he's listening.

"That girl." I take a deep breath. "She's really not one of us?"

"She wasn't a part of Black Wings," Jaxon says in a serious tone. "I didn't choose her among our members, but she is a part of us now. It's the only thing that will make her safe."

I curse silently.

Had I known that earlier, I wouldn't have thought that she was a poser or a Black Wings member who stupidly tried to upgrade her status by telling some fucked up lies.

"You have to accept her," Jaxon says. "You can't tell me that you're fine, Kellan. Physically, yes. But you're always angry." He sounds like he's speaking through gritted teeth, leaving me no room to argue. "I'm not dicing with death here just to hear that you're fucking destroying yourself over there. I'm not fucking coming back from Italy anytime soon, no matter what you do to make me. I hired Layla, so I will contact her if I need to. You don't want to pick up my call, anyway. I had to figure out a way to be assured that my brother wasn't going insane." With that said in full authority, Jaxon ends the call.

I roar at the ceiling, throwing my phone somewhere across the room with such fury that my body is shaking all over. My breathing is hard and fast. My chest is heaving up and down.

I can't believe what Jaxon has decided for me. I can't believe that I have to accept that girl, that I need to be friends with her. This is fucking ridiculous.

He said that he wanted to make sure that I wasn't going insane, but he just made it worse.

I lower myself to sit on my bed, my arms hanging on my thighs. While I'm still trying to breathe properly, my thoughts wander to the girl.

I remember the last thing I said to her.

"Get lost."

I clench my shaking fist, knowing that saying those words in front of our members would only cause her one thing.

Death.

L A Y L A

I can't breathe. I'm going to die.

Air is being sucked out of my lungs. My face is being pushed forcefully into the water. The grip on the back of my head is so painful, it makes me nauseous.

I choke, my arms flailing wildly and helplessly. I'm struggling to breathe for dear life.

Just when I think that I can't make it, the hand pulls my hair so roughly, my scalp is burning. I breathe the oxygen again, opening my eyes, which only hold fear.

I make out the shape of the water fountain before me. A strangled sob escapes from my mouth while two other Black Wings members secure my arms with their grip so that I won't be able to escape.

"You're trying to kill yourself, huh?" the cold voice echoes again in my ears.

My vision is already blurred because I'm slowly losing consciousness. Yet, I'm still trying to stand on my feet because I don't want to die.

I'd never been so close to death as I am right now.

They've been trying to drown me in the fountain located in the middle of the backyard of this mansion.

I squint. The guy who claimed himself as one of the Knights' right-hand man laughs at me. Everyone else laughs too, watching me. They're standing near the fountain and forming a circle to get a better look at me -- the joke.

I hear a girl scoff. "Told you. No one would believe your story."

I turn my head, only to find the girl named Brea crossing her arms over her chest and watching me with pity.

"Do you know her, Nina?" someone asks out loud, and now I know that her real name is not Brea.

Her boyfriend interrupts, "Not at all. We figured out that she lied, but she was stubborn and didn't listen to our warning." He looks at me in disgust.

"Is that true, Nathan?" another person asks, and now I also know that the boyfriend's real name is not Gio.

They weren't stupid enough to expose their real names if I ever got out of this place after spilling to me about their leaders.

But now that it's not possible for me to run away, there's nothing to lose for them.

Tears spill from my eyes as I remember my family. What have I gotten myself into? Will I never see them again? Will I really die here soon?

Kellan's words are like a stab to me. It doesn't just kill me inside, but it can actually kill me.

"Get lost."

Such words uttered by the King of Black Wings are enough to make the members take it as a death sentence for me.

"You said your name was Layla, didn't you?" the guy who has been ordering around asks me again, and nothing can describe how much I hate him.

He said his name was Luca and that he was Fenrir's most trusted person.

I remember Nina telling me that Fenrir is one of the Knights, and apparently, Luca here has been assigned by Fenrir to run the place while Fenrir himself is out for a search mission.

"So, Layla, you might be stupid for telling people that you're Kellan's caregiver, but your face is surely better than your brain," Luca says. "You're quite pretty."

My body shudders as he eyes me from head to toe like a hunter looking at his prey.

"Not pretty enough to fool any man," a girl shouts in the background.

Luca steps forward to me while I'm struggling to break free from the two people holding me. My clothes -- my cardigan and jeans -- are soaked because of all the splashing that happened while I was trying to get my face away from the water.

I'm already shuddering, but the way Luca stares down at me makes me shiver even more.

"Our king might want you dead," he says with the cockiest smirk. "But I'm sure that he won't mind if we use you for a while before that."

My heart jumps like a wild stag due to the fear consuming me.

"No," I stutter, my mind already figuring out what he has in mind. "Please, let me go."

Excitement becomes more obvious in his expression. "Not that easy, filthy little liar."

He tips my chin up with his finger. My lips tremble as another tear drops from my eye.

"I don't know," he whispers in a voice that makes me want to disappear from this world. "I'm thinking about turning you into a slave. What say you?"

That would be the worst way to live. My world crumbles.

"Say that again," a cold, threatening voice echoes through the night, and everyone suddenly turns dead silent.

Chills run down my spine as my gaze lands on the person I'm supposed to take care of.

Kellan Romero.

10

CHAPTER 10

L AYLA

The younger king of Black Wings enters the site. Everyone is on alert.

"Kellan," Luca's eyes widen as he watches Kellan walking toward him.

Kellan is blind, but he has excellent orientation of where he's heading, just by using his hearing and his other senses.

"I said..." Kellan clenches his jaw. "Say that again," he repeats in a menacing tone.

"Well," Luca begins nonchalantly, but I can hear the slight shake in his voice, a sign that he's intimidated but trying to hide it. "Since you practically announced that you wanted her gone, we were discussing how to get rid of her."

I can feel the air getting tense, like everyone is holding their breath. The silence that follows after is so gripping, you would even hear it if a pin dropped.

"We figured out that it would be better if we could make her our slave." As if he can sense that Kellan is about to counter that, Luca quickly adds, "I mean, she could be useful. You don't even have to feel her presence around. We will make sure that she won't bother you."

I never felt this low.

I feel so humiliated and degraded. Do they even see me as a person?

Kellan opens his mouth and what comes out surprises us all, "And what made you think that you shouldn't offer her to me first?" he asks in a cold voice.

Luca stares at him with a lost expression. "But you didn't want her anywhere near you."

Kellan steps forward again, his aura giving off unmistakable authority. "Well, apparently I wouldn't mind if she offered herself as my slave."

"Come on, man. You told her to get lost," a guy daringly shouts out loud, causing gasps and frantic whispers to fill the air.

Whoever just shouted doesn't value his life because their king can punish him in an instant. Luckily, he's hiding in the crowd.

Kellon scoffs, facing the crowd. "Right. I wasn't being completely fair to you. If you want her that much, we shall decide it in a fight. I'm your leader, and I'm now giving you equal opportunity."

The crowd goes even louder, wondering what that means.

"Whoever wins the fight will get her," Kellan says.

My heart almost stops. It will be better if they bury me alive. They don't even think of me as a human being. They're stomping my dignity and feelings like I'm a piece of trash.

Does this always happen every time they find an intruder inside Black Wings?

Everyone goes silent after that challenge from Kellan. No one moves. Luca doesn't move either even though I can see him balling his fist.

"Anyone?" Kellan asks.

Still, nobody dares fight him. Now, I see even more that everyone fears Kellan when it comes to one-on-one fights with him. The blind man is their martial arts trainer, and until now, I don't think that anyone here has ever beaten him.

"Well, it's clear now," Kellan says. He turns his back to us to walk away. "Follow me, Layla."

I freeze on the spot. I don't know what to do. I might have escaped a devil, but I might just be walking right to another one.

I'm supposed to take care of Kellan, but after what happened tonight, I don't think that I can trust him anymore.

"Now," he barks, making me jump in fear.

My mind is wondering if he's going to hurt me. But maybe it's better than staying here with these animals. Maybe I'll still have a chance to escape Kellan since he's blind.

Whispers and murmurs are still echoing around me when I finally take a step. My legs are shaking, and I'm afraid that I'm going to collapse.

Yet, I'm trying my best to walk. I follow Kellan back into the mansion that I will never be able to call home.

KELLAN

I feel her behind me when I step into my room.

"Close the door," I command, and she does as I say.

What happened in the backyard angers me, but I must admit that it was my fault.

I still haven't turned around. I expect her to talk first.

"What the hell is this?" her voice holds pain and anger, the tremor in it letting me know that she's trying to hide her fear too.

I turn around, which makes her immediately step back. It's bothering me that such a small movement from me causes her to draw back instantly. It's obvious that she sees me as a threat.

"What is happening?" she demands. Her choked sob makes me imagine the tears running down her face.

I can't blame her for crying. I heard the sound of water splashing when I found her in the backyard. They must have tried to drown her. Not to kill her, but to build the fear inside her.

"Your brother hired me as your caregiver," she says, "but then you told me to get lost. Why didn't you tell your brother about that, huh? And now you're expecting me to be your slave?" The frustration is evident in her voice.

I don't say anything yet. I know that she still has a lot to throw at me.

"This place is fucked up." Her choice of words makes me off guard because it's so different from the way she spoke to me for the first time in the basement.

That time, she sounded tentative, innocent. Right now, she sounds like a mess, like she's falling apart.

Her ragged breathing lets me know that she is about to break down.

"This place--" Her voice is shaking uncontrollably. "What the hell is this place? I don't want to be here. I don't belong here. Please, just let me go."

If she thinks that it will be that easy to just step out of this damn place, she's mistaken.

"Unfortunately," I say, and I do feel that word. I want her to leave this place too. "It's not possible anymore."

I step forward, and she retreats again. Her movement leads her to my bed. I follow her, causing her to be cornered against my bed.

"Once you step into this place, you can't get out of it," I say. "Either you're a part of us or you're dead. The only way for Black Wings members to leave this house is if they're on a mission."

"I don't want to be a part of it," she cries. "You guys are crazy. You're all evil."

Again, I can't blame her either for feeling that way because of what they did to her in the fountain. But silently, I'm angry at my brother for choosing a girl like her to be here. She doesn't belong in our world. She's not suited to be with us. She's pure.

"What do you guys do for a living? Killing people?" she asks, and I don't even know whether she asks that out of genuine curiosity or sarcastically. She sounds both.

I tower over her. "We might."

I can hear her faint gasp, and I can feel her trying to crawl away from me on the bed.

"What are you doing?" she stutters.

My blood starts to boil again. I don't know what's happening to me, but feeling her shaking due to her fear of me makes me angry.

I never thought that feeling someone shaking could annoy me this much. I felt people's fear of me when they fought me, but it never bothered me like this.

I draw my face closer to her, causing her to yelp. "Are you fucking crazy?" I hiss. "I'm not going to fucking touch you."

My words stop her movement, but then she cries softly. "I don't want to be anybody's slave. I'm not yours. I'm not a tool for you to use as you please, whether it be non-sexually or sex--"

"Shut the fuck up," I bite out. "Let me tell you something."

She's silent, and I can hear her swallow.

"I have no interest in you," I say. "You just happened to be stuck here, and there's no way out. I'm actually doing you a favor here. I doubt that there will be a place for you to sleep soundly other than this room, my room, after what happened tonight."

I didn't mean to make her remember what happened back there near the fountain, but she had to hear it.

There's no other place safer in this house for her than my bedroom.

Back there in the yard, I could hear their whispers when they thought about ways of using her. I could hear Luca's excitement and sick thought in his voice when he talked to her.

I'm blind, not fucking stupid.

No matter how much I don't want to admit it, the safest place for her here is where she is with me.

"So, we're going to do this," I say firmly. "You are here with me because you have no other choices. I am allowing it because my brother is being a pain in the ass. You're going to stay in this room, but you will do your best to make it feel like you don't even exist."

Silence falls.

She might be at a loss for words, but my idea is the only way for her to survive.

"This place is not for you, Layla," I speak in a low voice. "Black Wings is not where you belong. It's not your comfortable home where you can sleep soundly holding your unicorn. It's the place where you will hear gunshots and witness bloodshot when it's necessary."

She lets out an audible gasp. I can even hear the slap of her palm covering her mouth, as though she can't believe what I just said.

"I'm fucking blind, and I'm not your fucking hero," I make my point clearly. "So, it's up to you. You might want to try to escape and risk getting yourself killed. You might want to roam around the house where they will steal a chance to harass you, or you might want to stay here and be good, pretending like you don't even exist."

She doesn't say a word for a while, but then she whispers brokenly, "Why do you have to be so mean?"

I scoff. "You're welcome." I can't believe she forgot that I just saved her.

I walk away from my bed and head to the bathroom, leaving her to absorb everything that just happened to her.

It's only day one with Layla, and she has already given me a fucking headache.

LAYLA

I curl myself on the bed, leaning against the headboard as I hear the water running inside the bathroom. Kellan is taking a shower, and I'm here like a helpless girl.

What should I do?

While I'm hugging my knees, another lone tear falls to my cheek. I miss my family so much. I wonder what Nana and Archer are doing right now.

My phone has been taken from me, and I can't even call them. Even though I can't tell them what happened to me, I just want to hear their voices.

While I'm pondering in my thoughts, Kellan walks out of the bathroom with only a towel wrapped around his torso. The sight makes me let out a gasp, which causes Kellan to snap his head toward me with a scowl on his face.

He glares in my direction, his wet hair hanging loosely on his forehead. I'm restless because he looks angry, again.

"Did I not tell you to make it like you didn't even exist?" he reminds me in irritation.

"You're walking half naked," I counter.

He rolls his eyes.

"It's not my fault that you startled me," I say.

"It's not like I'm going to do something to you--" he stops mid-sentence and growls. "Fine."

It seems that he remembers what almost happened to me tonight. Despite still fuming, he snatches his jogger from the wardrobe and walks back into the bathroom. When he comes back, he's already wearing his pants.

I'm grateful that he didn't get naked and change clothes in front of me because that might make me feel uncomfortable.

I watch as he searches for something inside his wardrobe again, looking like he's trying to find a T-shirt to wear. His back is facing me, so I can see his massive black wings tattoo again. It indeed looks like actual wings, black with silver streaks, his identity as the king.

I find myself mesmerized by his tattoo again. It's beautiful.

"Stop staring," he snaps, making me taken aback. "I can't see it, but I can feel it."

I sigh, tearing my gaze away from him. I feel his movement toward the bed, and the next thing I know is that he dips into the bed, lying next to me, already wearing a black t-shirt.

He rolls on his side, facing the opposite direction. "Too bad that there's only one bed in this room, and that there's no fucking couch. Be grateful that I don't kick you out of my bed."

Again, his words sting.

Now that I think about it, he's actually doing something nice, but his words ruin it.

I travel my gaze around his neat bedroom. There's a recliner sofa near the bookshelves and a chair behind the desk, but none of them is suitable for someone to sleep on.

While my eyes focus on the bookshelves, I find many books lining inside it. I wonder if he reads braille books.

"Do you read--"

"Just let me fucking sleep," he interrupts before I can finish my question.

I stare down at myself, at the mess that I am. My clothes are damp because of what happened at the fountain, ruining the bedsheet where I'm sitting. But I don't care. I have no energy to move.

I feel drained, mentally and physically. My body no longer feels cold. Maybe it has been numb for a while.

But then, I can get sick if I stay like this, so after mustering all the energy left in me, I get off the bed and walk toward the bathroom to wash myself.

11

CHAPTER 11

K ELLAN

I could barely get enough fucking sleep last night.

While I was lying in my bed, I couldn't stop thinking about Layla. I knew for sure that her clothes were soaked because of the incident at the fountain, and when she finally decided to take a shower, I did let out a sigh of relief.

She didn't have her suitcase with her yesterday, so I knew that she didn't have any clothes to change into. I purposely left the bathrobe hanging behind the bathroom door, and I guess she took that.

I just couldn't imagine her sleeping beside me without any clothes on. She didn't seem like a girl who would be comfortable doing that despite the fact that I was blind.

The night was getting worse when she started crying. She might think that I didn't notice it, but I could hear her sniffling, and it was fucking annoying. I knew that she had just left her family and that she was now stuck in this place that felt like hell to her, but goddammit I hate it when girls or women cry.

Not that I cared.

Or was it annoying because I fucking cared?

Now as the morning comes, I splash the water from the sink onto my face. My head is pounding. I brush my teeth, but I still can't stop thinking about the girl who is now sleeping in my bed.

My brain is trying to figure out what I will do today with her being around. Her existence is already annoying me this much, I wonder how I will survive the following weeks -- or worse, months. Jaxon better be fucking coming back here as soon as possible so that we can talk. I have to persuade him to send Layla away, but with the way we always argue, we will only end up fighting.

Maybe he's right. I can't fucking control my anger. But then again, he's not the one with disability.

I step out of my bathroom, ready to have my morning jog. The sooner I can escape Layla, the better.

Layla's voice surprises me when I'm about to open the door of my bedroom.

"Where are you going?" she asks.

I turn around, hoping that she will notice the irritation written on my face.

"Morning jog," I say.

I'm about to turn around when she interrupts, "Wait. Please, don't leave me just yet." Her voice holds so much vulnerability, and I can't help but feel bad. She's still trying to figure out how to adjust to this new situation.

I give her my attention again, waiting for her to say more.

"How will I have my meal?" she asks, and I figure out that she's hungry.

She didn't ask about the place where she could have breakfast in this house, which means that she's still afraid of getting out of this room.

"You'll get it," I say.

I'd already thought about it last night.

"Someone will bring it for you."

She's silent, but I can feel her uneasiness.

"Don't worry," I say. "It won't be the guys from last night. You'll get to know her soon."

She sighs in relief, knowing that it will be a girl who will come to this room.

"What about you?" she asks with a hint of curiosity in her voice. She must have seen the confusion in my face, because the next thing she says is, "I mean, I know that you can have breakfast anywhere in this house, but I just want to know your usual routines. Do you eat in the kitchen or dining room? Or do you prefer to have your meal inside your room? What about your schedules? Do you have a martial arts practice during the day? When do you train the fighters? Do you go out--"

"I thought I made it clear that I didn't need a goddamn caregiver," I snap, not wanting to hear the rest of her questions.

She doesn't respond to my harsh statement right away, but after seconds pass, she says fiercely, "Then what do you expect me to do?"

I can hear the frustration in her voice.

"Do you really want me to go crazy, being imprisoned in this room like a lost wounded animal? Why don't you just tell everyone in here that I am indeed your caregiver hired by your brother? If you had done so, I wouldn't have been picked by them and they wouldn't see me as a slave that they could just use and trash once you're bored with me." Her sob suddenly breaks, letting me know how much that thought has been haunting her.

I can hear her fear all over again in her voice, and my fist instantly shakes with rage again. I hate how she is affecting me this much. I don't know how to respond to her demand yet, so being the cruel man that I am, I turn my back to her.

"Kellan." Layla grabs my arm.

Her touch almost makes me explode. I don't like being touched, literally, by anyone. One who knows me better will be smart enough to maintain distance from me.

But Layla's touch is even worse. She's shaking, begging for help. To me, she feels fragile as a glass. She makes me want to pull her into me, but at the same time, I want to push her away because I'm afraid that she will shatter.

What the fuck is wrong with me? This girl is making me crazy.

While I'm trying my best to hold my anger, I turn my head again. I can't see her expression when she looks at my face, but whatever it is that she sees, it gives her hope because she says, "Please. I really need your help."

"Make it quick." I can only utter those harsh words.

I know that once again, I made her heart sink, contrary to my intention of helping her.

"My suitcase," she stutters, "the guard outside didn't give it back to me after inspecting it. I really need it. My clothes are in there. My stuff--"

Those words are enough for me, so without waiting for her to finish her sentence, I step out of my room and shut the door behind me, leaving her alone.

L A Y L A

I hear the door being knocked, and once I open it, I am greeted with a girl.

She looks around the same age as me. She has shoulder-length hair -- brown colored -- and she has pretty green eyes.

She smiles at me, and I can already feel her kindness.

When I focus on the tray of food she's holding, I quickly open the door wider to let her in. I watch as she places the tray on Kellan's desk.

"Thank you so much." I approach her, grateful that she did come to bring me food.

I'm expecting her to say something back, but then she points at the door, as though she's trying to tell me that she still has something else for me. A moment later, she drags my suitcase into the room, and huge relief washes over me, I feel like I can burst into tears.

I was worried that I had lost my belongings.

"Thank you. You don't know how much this means to me." I want to hug her, and since she doesn't show any reluctance, I wrap my arms around her.

When I pull away, I see the same happiness skating on her face. This girl seems like a genuine person. I feel like I can be her friend.

"Did Kellan tell you about this?" I ask.

The answer is clear, but I just want to hear it from her. She only nods, and I assume that she's not a talkative person.

"I'm Layla, by the way." I stretch my arm for a handshake, which she accepts. "And you are?" I raise my eyebrows.

To my surprise, instead of answering my question, she pulls out a pile of small note papers and a pen from her pants pocket. My curiosity kicks in as she starts writing something. When she shows me what it is, my heart sinks.

I'm Zoe. Nice to meet you, Layla!

I'm a mute, by the way. I can't talk. I hope you don't mind talking to me like this.

I shake my head and smile. "Of course. I'm so happy to meet you, Zoe. Thank you for helping me out."

To answer your question, yes, Kellan did tell me to do these things for you.

Honestly, it's rare to see him do something like this.

"Is he a nice person?" I ask. "Please be honest."

Zoe shakes her head in amusement.

Sometimes he acts like a pain in the ass, but he's actually a good person. Don't worry.

I let out a sigh of relief. Talking to Zoe is already making me much calmer. I need someone like her in a place like this.

"My job is to take care of him," I say. "But he doesn't let me."

A frown touches her lips.

Why?

"I don't know." I shrug. "I'm pretty sure that he found me annoy-ing."

This time, Zoe shakes her head in disagreement.

Don't let that get into your head. Please, don't give up. I think he needs someone like you. Just let me know if I can help you with anything.

There's so much more I want to hear from her about her sentence, but I decide to focus on one point first.

"I really appreciate your help," I say. "Can you tell me more about him and this place? He's blind. How does he usually get help around here?"

With enthusiasm, Zoe writes me, and her answers are long.

Kellan has been living here since he was born. He lost his eyesight when he was only 9 years old in a car crash that killed his parents and his sister. Since then, he kind of changed into someone who was always angry. Many people saw him, and still see him, as a lost cause because none of them knows him better. He's traumatized, and not many people can understand that. Please, don't give up on him. Behind his harsh exterior is a kind and caring person.

As for his daily needs, he usually takes his meals in the kitchen unless he's not in the mood and wants to bring the food to his bedroom. All Black Wings members do their laundry by themselves, but it doesn't apply to Kellan. My father does that for him.

I ponder in thought. Zoe's father might not have to do that anymore because it's now my job.

Curiosity builds up inside me. "I'm sorry for asking this, but what does your father do? And what about you? In which part of the house do you two live in?"

It's very tempting for me to sleep in her place. It sounds better than here, on the same bed with Kellan. But I don't want to barge into her privacy -- I just met her.

My father is a tattoo artist. He does the tattoo for Black Wings leaders and members. Sometimes, I help him with that.

We live in the basement but not the one where the boxing ring is. It's another basement.

I remember Nina telling me about the Black Wings tattoo that can only be crafted by two artists. Apparently, they're Zoe's father and herself. They must be so talented that no other artists can copy what they do. It's because of them that Black Wings can maintain their tattoo exclusivity. Nobody can have a Black Wings identity unless it's made by them.

Zoe and her father must be considered very important for Black Wings. It's no wonder that she seems close to Kellan and that Kellan trusts her.

I can't help but give her another hug. "Thank you for coming here. I hope we can be good friends."

She smiles sweetly, returning my hug. Then she writes again on another note.

Of course :)

Anyway, I have to go help my father again now. Before I go, there's something else I want to give you.

I frown, wondering what it is. Zoe reaches for something from the other pocket of her pants. My eyes widen as she hands me a phone. It's not mine, but it looks brand new.

I read a note from her.

This is from Jaxon. He'll call you.

I'm sorry that your phone was taken. Black Wings members are not supposed to have personal phones other than the ones given by their leaders, and not everyone in here can have them.

I take the phone from her. "Thank you."

I'm glad that I can finally talk to Jaxon.

I never expected that I would be shoved into this kind of dangerous environment when I first accepted this job.

Hopefully, Jaxon can give me an explanation.

My heart leaps with delight as I think that I can talk to Nana and Archer again. I remember Archer's number, so even though I don't have my phone with me anymore, I can still call them by using this phone from Jaxon.

Zoe writes to me again.

I'll see you again.

I nod as she gives me another reassuring smile. She excuses herself, and I watch as she steps out of the room and closes the door.

12

CHAPTER 12

L AYLA

I plop myself on the bed, going through my new phone with excitement. I know that everything I do with this phone -- all my calls and all my messages -- may be tracked by Black Wings, but I don't care.

I proceed with setting up the phone first, including putting my fingerprint and passcode for security. I know that they can do anything, but this is just for precaution in case the horrible guys out there suddenly want to take it again. The thought of them harassing me still makes me think twice before going out of this room. My heart sinks as I realize all over again that I am no more than a prisoner here.

Just as I'm about to dial Archer's number, the phone rings. I stare blankly at the unknown number showing on the screen, wondering if it's Jaxon.

I swallow, answering the call. "Hello?"

"Layla," a man's voice echoes in my ear.

It's Jaxon.

I have so many questions in my head that I don't even know what I should say to him. Before I can make up my mind, Jaxon is already speaking again.

"I may not have enough time because I'm in a hurry, but I have to talk to you about Kellan." There are sounds of people speaking in the background, distinctly, so I'm guessing that he's in a public space but currently excusing himself to make this call. "How is he?" he asks, and I can hear concern in his voice. "How is my brother?"

I want to say that Kellan is being a pain in the ass, but then, I decide to choose the words wisely. I'm talking to the first heir, the King of Black Wings.

"To be honest," I begin. "He's a difficult person. Did you even tell him that I was going to be his caregiver? Because it didn't seem like he agreed to it."

Jaxon sighs and then curses. "I had no other choices. He's pulling away from me, and I just want to know that he's okay. He needs someone to take care of him, no matter how hard it is for him to admit that."

I remember very clearly that Kellan hated to feel that he was incapable. That was why he told me to get lost.

"I know that you paid me in full amount, but I don't think that I can--"

"Listen to me," he cuts me off. "I don't care about the money. You don't even have to return it should anything happen before the contract ends."

Jaxon sounds pissed, and it makes me think twice before crossing him again.

"My brother has been in agony since he lost his eyesight," Jaxon says, "and the environment around him -- that fucking house -- is not good enough for him to heal. There are only a few people I can trust there, and they don't have the capacity to give him the help that I want."

I listen intently, sensing that what he's about to say is going to be important.

"Kellan is constantly angry with everything, but mostly with what happened to him. I don't think that he'll ever accept the fact that he's blind and that it's permanent," Jaxon says heartbreakingly, I can almost feel the pain myself. "He's angry that he can't be normal. He thinks that he's incapable, which is far from the truth. I always knew that he had a protective nature since he was a kid, so I taught him martial arts. It helped him a lot. He learned so hard. I taught him, and I taught him, until he became even better than I was."

Jaxon sounds like he's speaking through gritted teeth, like it hurts him to the core that his brother is suffering.

"Right now, he can fight better than me, and I can't be more proud of that. But it's not enough."

I swallow, waiting for him to say more.

"He doesn't let go of the grudge inside him, and he always thinks less of himself. Waiting for him to fall apart is like a ticking time bomb. I don't want to lose my brother," he emphasizes every word of the last sentence.

I hear the sound of a gunshot from the other side of the line, and my heart almost stops. Shouts are ringing, and someone tells Jaxon to leave the place.

"Shit," Jaxon curses in a low voice.

It sounds like chaos over there. People are screaming. Someone is crying. More gunshot sounds are heard.

"I have to go," Jaxon says. "Please stay with Kellan. Help him see that he's not the person he thinks he is. You have a family who went through a similar experience, and you fucking know how I feel. Just bring his light back. Bring my brother back." Another curse, and just like, that the call abruptly ends.

My heart is racing, and I realize that I've been panting. I don't know what is happening with Jaxon right now, but I hope that he makes it out alive. He's the only one who can help me out of this place.

While I'm trying to compose myself, I ball my fist tightly. I can't back down now. I have a family that I have to return to, so I'm going to nail this job whatever happens.

Because Jaxon Romero doesn't want me to give up on his brother.

Thankfully, the call with Nana and Archer went smoothly. I just wanted to let them know that I was doing okay and to make sure that they were doing all right without me. In their mind, I was studying at Texas Tech University, and luckily, I could answer their questions about my living apartment, my studies, and my roommate without having to make it suspicious.

I transferred a portion of the money that I got from Jaxon to them. I lied to them, telling them that it was excess money from the loan added to my salary from my previous part-time job. What they didn't know yet was that I was going to transfer more money.

Today, it's my third day inside this Black Wings mansion. As soon as I finish changing my clothes in the bathroom after taking my morning shower, I see Kellan sitting on the recliner sofa beside the bookshelf.

Judging from the sight of him lying there with his eyes closed and earphones plugged in his ears, it seems that he fell asleep again while he was listening to music.

I sigh. I want to ask him about breakfast, but he looks so peaceful sleeping there that I don't dare wake him up.

Yesterday, Zoe brought me meals three times a day. But today, I'm not sure if it's going to be the same.

I take my new phone from the nightstand to check if Jaxon has replied to the text I sent him last night.

I need your help. I don't feel safe in this mansion because I'm not a member of Black Wings. They think I'm an intruder because I don't have any Black Wings tattoo. Can you clear that up?

My shoulders sag in disappointment because there's no reply yet. He hasn't even read it.

My mind is telling me that something bad has indeed happened to him during his mission, but worrying will do nothing to help me. I just hope that he will respond as soon as possible so that my worry will be eased.

I glance at Kellan again, thinking that I shouldn't be depending on other people that much. My job here is to take care of Kellan, and I can't do that if I'm being a crybaby myself. Besides, if I go downstairs to get food for Kellan, they can't possibly harm me.

With that in mind, I head to the door, preparing to get food for myself and Kellan. We can just have our meals inside his room.

When my hand touches the door handle, I glance back one last time at Kellan and find him still sleeping soundly on the sofa. I step out of the room and close the door behind me softly.

I hope that the hallway will be deserted, but that would be too good to be true.

While I'm trying to find my way to the kitchen, I pass some guys and girls who automatically snap their heads toward me as soon as I walk by. Their gazes make the hair on the back of my neck stand.

The atmosphere here hasn't changed at all. It's still as horrible as the night they were trying to drown me.

The air around me feels like it's made of sin. No kindness. No empathy. Just evil.

I can hear their whispers.

"Look. That's Kellan's slave."

"Do you think that he touched her? I don't think he ever touched a girl."

I can feel the girls' jealousy all over the air. While I'm trying to ignore all their acquisitions about me, one comment makes my pulse quicken.

"Look. It's the girl without the tattoo."

Fear builds up inside me again. I want to run for my life. I don't belong here. They're supposed to kill me. I don't know if Kellan claiming me as his slave would save me anymore.

It's not that difficult to find the kitchen because, at this hour, that's where everyone practically comes and goes.

Many kinds of food are already prepared on the giant kitchen island, where everyone can just grab a plate. The sooner I can get out of the kitchen, the better. I take a tray and start to prepare the food for Kellan and myself.

A whistle catches me off guard. I snap my head toward the source of the voice, and to my horror, Luca is staring at me.

13

CHAPTER 13

L AYLA

Luca crosses his arms over his chest. "Look who we have here. Kellan's slave, who is apparently a girl without the tattoo."

Everyone's attention is immediately on me, even more so than before.

I try to ignore him, focusing on pouring mushroom soup into a bowl. My hand is slightly shaking when I proceed to grab the toasts. I pray in my heart that he will just go away, but unfortunately, he walks in my direction instead.

I'm about to grab the drinks when I collide with someone's chest. I almost drop the tray. I look up, only to find Luca looking down at me with a smug grin. He's accompanied by two guys, who stand on each of his sides.

"Well, then." He raises an eyebrow mockingly. "Did he treat you better than we did?"

Chills run through my skin as I remember what this man has done to me. They laugh.

"Come on," his friend says. "You need to tell us if he gets bored of you already so that we can start teaching you a lot of wonderful things without crossing him."

"Unless our king wants to share." The other guy smirks. "It's risky." He tsks. "But maybe it's worth a try."

"Careful, guys," someone interrupts, and when I turn my head, I see a tanned guy with curly hair shooting a warning look at the three of them. "As far as I remember, Kellan doesn't like to share. Do you not remember the way he challenged us to fight him over Layla? I would think a million times before going against him."

My chest is filled with relief. Finally, someone is trying to knock some sense into them.

Luca's face hardens as he thinks about it carefully.

Before Luca can make a move toward me, the guy who just stood up for me grabs my arm, dragging me away. "Come, Layla. I'll help you get the drinks."

I glance back at Luca and his friends. He mutters something under his breath before the three of them leave the kitchen. I sigh in relief.

"Thanks," I say to the person who just saved me.

He helps me put two bottles of water onto the tray I'm holding. "You're welcome." He smiles, and I'm thankful that there's kindness greeting me. "I'm Marco, by the way."

I follow him as he leads me back into the hallway. I thought that he would go with me upstairs, but then he lightly pushes me toward an area under the staircase, surprising me. He corners me against the wall but still maintains a safe distance from me, as though he's trying to tell me that he's not going to hurt me.

"You have to be careful, Layla," he says. "What's a girl like you doing in a place like this?"

I huff. "Well, surprise. I'm indeed Kellan's caregiver. He just doesn't want to admit it."

Marco frowns. "That's the truth?" His mouth twitches in disapproval. "What a fucking jerk."

"Do you think that everyone is going to believe me?" I ask genuinely.

Marco stares down, as if he's deep in thought. Then he returns his gaze to me. "I don't know." There's disappointment in his voice. "I'm sorry, but I don't think that they will, unless you have a tattoo."

"Can I not work as a caregiver for Black Wings leader without being a part of it?" I ask. "I mean, I don't even want to be a member."

"Not a chance," Marco says truthfully. "The rules here are very clear. Non-members are not allowed to enter the property. It's not negotiable."

I swallow.

"Stay away from Luca," Marco says. "He's dangerous. He's no good for you."

I laugh humorlessly. "I'm very aware of that. Do you know him well?"

Marco shakes his head. "Not really, but enough to know what kind of person he is. My brother is the one close to him. I'm sorry, he took part in mocking you just now."

I can see Marco's anger radiating from his body, and it's flattering that he cares about me, unlike most people here.

"If nobody here won't believe my story unless I have a tattoo, what makes you believe me?" I ask, and when he gives me a questioning look, I quickly add, "Not that I have a problem with that. I just want to know why because it means so much to me."

Marco's smile is back on his face. "Because I know how it felt."

I squint at him.

"Because I was once like you, Layla," he says. "I saw you when you first stepped into this place. You looked lost, so very lost. You didn't want to be here. You're not an intruder, and I knew it the moment I saw you for the first time."

His words almost make me cry. He's the only person in this place who believes me so easily.

Even Kellan couldn't do that.

"I was also like that," he says. "I was here because I was worried about my brother. He sent a lot of money, but my family never figured out what he actually did. I did tons of research and finally found out about Black Wings. I was worried that he was involved in something dangerous, and it turned out that my fear was right. Now, I'm stuck in this place too because I was looking for him."

His story is painful, and I feel sad for him.

"I'm so sorry," I whisper. "I'm sorry that this happened to you."

He shakes his head again. "I'm okay now. I can survive. It's you I'm worried about. You're not supposed to be here. This place will ruin you. Kellan is blind, but he's a dangerous man. Tell me, did he touch you?"

Something glints in his eyes -- a hint of possessiveness -- but I don't want to think too much about it.

"No, he didn't," I say.

Marco smiles. "Good. Just let me know if you need anything." He suddenly kisses my cheek, startling me.

When I look up at him, he only gives me a playful smirk.

"Where the hell have you been?" Kellan's loud voice snaps at me the moment I come back into his room.

I close the door behind me with my foot and place the tray of food on the nightstand.

Kellan glares in my direction, already standing up with his arms crossed over his chest.

His temper makes my head spin, so I answer with the same irritated tone. "As far as I remember, you were sleeping on that chair, so forgive me if I didn't want to wake you up," I say sarcastically. "I also remember someone telling me to make it like I don't even exist in this room."

His lips form into a thin line. "I was planning to ask you to come downstairs with me for breakfast."

My mouth hangs open. Slight guilt sips into me.

He actually thought about that, and I didn't expect it.

"Well, you don't have to do that anymore." My voice softens. "I brought our breakfast here."

He sniffs, and I don't know why, but the sight is amusing.

"Yeah. It smells good," he mumbles. "Is it--"

"Mushroom soup," I finish for him, guessing that it's the food he's asking about because of its mouthwatering aroma.

I walk up to him with the bowl of mushroom soup in my hands. I place it on his desk, and he immediately sits behind it.

"Someone's hungry." I chuckle lightly. "Is it your favorite food?"

Kellan doesn't even bother to deny it, so I guess that it is.

He takes the spoon and carefully feeds himself, but then he suddenly splatters it, making me yelp in surprise.

"Careful. It's still hot--"

"Did you put fucking corn in it?" he hollers, it's almost comical to look at.

"What?" I echo.

"Corn," he hisses.

A light bulb pops in my head. He freaking hates corn.

"I didn't know that you didn't like it," I blurt. "I wasn't the one who cooked it either, so it wasn't my fault."

He drops the spoon onto the tray, causing it to clatter with a loud sound, echoing in the room. His disappointment is all over his face, so I can't help but feel empathy.

"You can still eat it, you know. I can help you with that." I approach him, but his body language is not so welcoming.

"What do you mean?" he asks in a curious tone.

"I can feed you and make sure that the corn won't get into the spoon," I say.

He doesn't say anything right away, but one would cower under his angry stare. "Are you saying that you're going to fucking feed me?"

"Come on," I say. "Don't be baby. It's not the time to argue. You're hungry. You're starving for your favorite food--"

"I'm not letting you feed me," he says with implacable authority.

I almost growl in frustration. "Then you can say bye-bye to your mushroom soup. How are you going to eat it without my help? How would you separate the tiny corns-- my God, everybody likes corns. How in the world do you not like it--"

"Shut the fuck up," he barks to make me stop talking. "Goddammit, your voice is annoying."

I zip my mouth, trying to be professional. Working with a disabled person -- especially one with a temper like his -- requires never-ending patience.

We just argued like we were still in kindergarten, and I can't help but feel shame.

"So, are you going to let me feed you or not?" I ask, unable to hide my irritation.

He thinks for long seconds and then says in such a low voice, I almost can't hear it. "Just this once."

I try to muffle my laughter, taking the spoon in my hand. It's not every time that I hear a mafia leader admitting his defeat.

"Why didn't you just tell me that you were hungry when you woke up?" I ask. "You could have had your breakfast earlier."

"Because I knew that you would be hungry too and that you needed me to feel safe downstairs to get your breakfast," he says, shocking me with his honesty. "I was waiting for you, but you took a goddamn long shower. I fell asleep while waiting for you."

I'm at a loss for words. Maybe Kellan Romero isn't as bad as he seems.

I smile, but he can't see it.

"Here comes the food," I hum.

He willingly opens his mouth. He swallows the soup, closing his eyes in satisfaction.

"No corn, right?" I ask.

He opens his eyes and sighs. "No corn," he whispers, making me smile again.

He looks contented now but still looks deadly. I wonder if a smile ever touches his lips again. That thought makes me want to work hard to earn it.

As I continue feeding him, I playfully try the airplane gesture. It fails miserably, only earning a deadly stare from him. I'm sure that his enemy would flee in an instant if they saw it, but it doesn't affect me. I laugh, really hard. My laughing makes him freeze, so I abruptly stop my laughter.

"What?" I whisper.

"You're laughing," he says with a frown on his lips. "I think it's the first time I heard you laugh since you came here."

Now that I think about it, he's right.

I didn't think that I would ever laugh again here, but I did it.

The fact catches me by surprise too.

"I guess so."

"It's annoying," he scowls, and I think that I'm going to have a headache again. "Your laughter is so annoying."

Why does he have to ruin it?

I scoff, and the rest of my feeding him goes quiet.

14

CHAPTER 14

KELLAN

It's been several weeks since Layla came into this house, and her existence is making me crazy.

I can't stop thinking about how she snuggles on the bed beside me, her annoying singing every time she takes a shower, and her voice every time she opens her mouth.

It's not like I haven't heard a girl's voice before, but there's something about her voice that can't leave my mind. Even the sound of her sigh and yawn are haunting me.

Why the hell does she have to sound so lively -- and sometimes so fierce -- but at the same time, I can also hear her softness and vulnerability? It doesn't make any sense.

If this is what it feels to live with a girl, I'd rather lock myself up in a mountain and live with a fucking bear.

Another thing that I can't fight is her scent. Goddammit, her scent... I wish I never knew it. She smells like delicate flowers and sweets. I fucking hate it.

In my case, there's only a thin line between hating it and being obsessed with it. I hate it because I can't control how much it affects me. I don't want to admit that I'm a fucking creep, but I would be lying if I said that I didn't try to sniff her scent on the bedsheet when she took a shower.

Today, I'm taking my evening jog around the house when I feel someone's footsteps rushing behind me. I don't need to face the person to know who it is. The footsteps belong to Layla.

She's panting and trying to catch up with my pace because her steps are way too short compared to mine.

"Kellan," her voice greets me again, and annoyingly, my heart almost skips a beat.

I don't know what the hell is wrong with me. Why is my heart not being cooperative every time she's trying to warm up to me?

The wind blows through my skin, and I close my eyes, inhaling the air. The smell of the grass is overwhelming -- it's going to rain soon. I can smell the rain even though it hasn't started yet. We need to go back inside as soon as possible because I hate being in the rain.

Unfortunately, Layla is about to waste my time again.

I turn around to face her. She abruptly stops her movement, and I can feel her staring up at me.

"You haven't told me about your practice schedule tonight," she asks, still trying to catch her breath. "Will you be in the boxing ring again tonight? What about dinner? When do you prefer to have it?"

"What the fuck are you doing?" I snap, trying to control my emotions. "Why do you have to always follow me? I'm not a fucking child. I can take care of myself, and I was doing just fine before you came here. How many times do I have to tell you that you're fucking annoying?"

Layla is silent, and I realize that my words might be too harsh.

"I'm sorry." To my surprise, she utters those words. She indeed sounds guilty. "I didn't mean to barge into your personal space. I didn't mean to disturb your privacy. I just--" she stumbles upon her words, sounding like she's in trouble. "There's something I..."

I frown, waiting for her explanation. Strangely, my pulse quickens, like I'm afraid that something bad is actually happening to her.

She's still trying to find the right words when the rain starts to pour down on us. I curse. The more seconds pass, the harder the rain falls.

I stomp away from Layla to find a place to shield us from the rain. It will be too far to go back into the house because we're in the farthest spot in the backyard. If I didn't hate rain so much, I would consider that option.

Before I know it, I'm running toward a gazebo standing not so far away from where we are. I remember precisely where it is, so I don't have any problem finding it even though I'm blind. I know every part of this property like the back of my hand.

The harsh pouring of the rain against my body is already making my blood boil. The sound of it falling hard is blocking my hearing.

Fucking rain. I fucking hate it.

I stop under the gazebo, panting. Layla arrives beside me. She's also panting, but not as hard as I am.

"What's wrong?" she asks with concern, noticing that this is not a normal reaction to the weather.

I shut my eyes, clenching my fists tightly on my sides. "I hate it." My voice sounds like a rasp. I open my eyes again.

"What?"

"The rain."

For a long moment, none of us speaks. Only the sound of the rain falling hard echo around us.

"Why?" Layla finally asks again. She sounds genuinely worried, which breaks down my walls a little bit.

"It makes me feel helpless," I say, surprising myself that I'm actually admitting it out loud.

This girl is slowly making me let out my pent-up emotions. I don't even know how she does that.

Layla doesn't push for more elaboration, but the words are already on the tip of my tongue.

"I hate how the rain falls on my body," I say. "It's fucking harsh, like it's trapping all my senses. I'm already blind, so I don't like feeling it."

She stays silent, and I continue, "The rain also washes away all the other smells and scents. I feel like all my clues have disappeared. It also impairs my hearing ability because all I can hear is the sound of it pouring harshly all around me."

Now, all I can hear is indeed the sound of the rain. If Layla didn't stand next to me, I wouldn't be able to hear her.

"That sounds so gloomy," she says, making my brows furrow. "On the other hand," she continues with a cheerful voice, "I see a rain as something good. Happiness."

I can imagine the big smile on her face as she says that.

"I like to play and dance in the rain," she says. "You're right. All we can feel and hear is the rain itself, but it feels liberating, like we don't have to think about anything else. We shut up the entire world, and we can just do anything we want."

I feel her moving toward the rain, and that makes me alert. What the hell is she going to do?

Her laughter rings in the air as she allows herself to get drenched in the rain. She sounds so happy, like a little girl.

"Oh God. It feels so good." She squeals between laughter.

She then hums, moving. The sound of water splattering on the ground lets me know that she's twirling and dancing, like the world doesn't matter.

"Are you crazy?" I hiss.

"Come on." She approaches me and takes my hands, trying to drag me into the rain. Her fingers are cold, but she doesn't sound like the coldness bothers her.

My hands are slightly shaking, and it's fucking embarrassing.

"It's okay." Her soft voice is so close to me, trying to calm me. "I'll show you something so that you don't have to be afraid of the rain anymore."

The idea sounds so tempting. I somehow manage to push my ego aside. Slowly, I walk off from the gazebo, letting the rain attack me.

As usual, I feel trapped, especially since it's falling so hard right now.

"Easy," she says gently, still holding my hands tightly.

I feel like a lost and wounded animal, and she is my only anchor.

"You think too much," she says. "Just this once, don't think about anything else. You're okay. You're safe."

I swallow, feeling like her soft voice is the only light for me in this darkness.

I look up toward the sky as drops of rain fall onto my face.

"Can you feel it?" she asks, still with the same gentleness. "Feel the rain. Breathe it. It's not going to harm you. It's not trying to trap you. It wants to wash away all your pain."

I don't know why I'm letting someone speak to me about something so intense and emotional, but I want to believe her words. I'm now in the middle of conquering one of my biggest fears. I'm sure that I would become even worse if I didn't believe her words.

I close my eyes and inhale deeply, sucking as much air as I need into my lungs. Instead of breathing fear, I'm trying to feel what it really is.

Fresh. Slightly cold. But refreshing.

It doesn't smell so bad anymore. It's the smell of nature, and it's not my enemy. If it's true that it's trying to wash away all my pain, I will completely let it.

There's nothing I need more than to let go of my pain, the pain that has been torturing me since the day my world shattered.

When I open my eyes again, a lone tear rolls down my cheek, and I'm grateful that she can't see it. It would look just like another drop of rain running down my face.

"Dance with me," she asks teasingly, and I can imagine her plastering a smile.

A sudden urge to see how she looks when she smiles consumes me. How does she look when she smiles?

"Come on." A giggle bursts from her mouth as she touches my shoulder while still holding my hand with her other hand.

She starts to guide me through the steps, and then we're dancing in the rain.

She dances so effortlessly. I don't think that she knows what she's doing because this is the silliest movement that I've ever done in my life. But she doesn't give a damn. She dances like nothing else matters.

Just like she said, the rain is making us forget the entire world and letting us do any goddamn thing we want.

She laughs, making a twirl and holding my hand. The sound of her laughter combined with the sound of the rain falling is the most beautiful thing I've ever heard in my life, and I don't ever want this to end.

My thought catches me off guard, and I abruptly stop my movement, startling her. The rain has gradually turned into drizzling. It's not falling hard anymore, and my other senses start to grow back.

"Kellan?" Layla asks. "What's wrong?"

A thunder suddenly strikes, causing her to scream and stumble into my chest. I automatically hold her in my arms, and in this very moment, I can feel how hard her heart is beating against mine, how hard our hearts are beating.

"Sorry," she stutters, quickly pulling away from me.

An awkward silence falls, so I speak to her, "You still haven't told me why you're following me today. You were saying that there was something--"

I can't continue my sentence because I don't know the answer. I can feel her hesitance, and I'm trying my best to hold my anxiety.

"Well," she starts, sounding like she feels ashamed about what she's about to say. "Actually, I've been following you around because I still don't feel safe roaming around this house alone."

Anger crawls into me like a sickening disease.

"Especially around mealtime," she continues. "I know that you saved me and that no one would want to cross you, but those guys are such jerks, they are still trying to intimidate me while they can--"

I can't hear the rest. With rage consuming my body, I walk away from her and storm back in the direction of the house.

"Kellan," she shouts, rushing up to catch me. "Wait."

The sound of her shoes stomping on the ground and making the water splash echoes in my ear, but I don't stop. I keep striding toward the house.

I'm not your fucking hero.

I remember the words I said to her, the words I've been trying to plant in my head because there's no way that I could be that to her.

"Kellan, please," Layla demands, following me. "What's wrong with you?" Her voice almost cracks. Frustration is evident in her tone.

I'm not your fucking hero.

Those words echo again and again in my head, taunting me, mocking me. What my heart wants, however, is far from that. Yet, the truth hits me hard. I can't be.

The fear of failing someone, of losing someone after trying to protect them is still very much in my heart. I failed once even though it almost cost my life.

I'm fucking blind now. I'm not destined to be a hero. Her hero. And it fucking makes me mad.

I'm so angry and out of control that I almost slip while walking down the small stairs on the way from the backyard. Layla quickly catches me, grabbing my arm, but the ground is so slippery that she falls.

I pant, my eyes wide in shock. I'm gripping the small railing with my other hand. I'm alright, but Layla...

She fell, and there was nothing I could do to prevent that. She was protecting me.

"Ouch," she hisses in pain.

Blood rushes to every vein in my body, and my heart feels like it's about to burst out of my chest. It's just a small step, so she can't be injured badly, but it doesn't make me less panic.

"I think I just sprained my ankle," she says, sounding like she's trying to hide her pain.

I explode. "What the fuck did you think you just do?" My voice booms, I can even hear her gasp in shock. "Did you even think before you did that? I told you countless times to fucking leave me alone. Did you ever fucking get what I said? For fuck's sake, just go away."

My chest rises and falls because of the way I speak, so brutally and mercilessly.

The sound of raindrops and my heavy breathing is the only thing that we can hear, until her cries break.

"Why are you doing this?" The pain in her voice lets me know that my words were like daggers to her heart.

My fist is shaking when I hear her crying. Her sadness feels like knives slicing my soul.

I grit my teeth, holding my fucked up emotions so that I wouldn't create more damage. I walk off, leaving her alone

15

CHAPTER 15

LAYLA

When I woke up this morning, Kellan was already gone. After what happened the day before, we hadn't spoken to each other again.

Last night, Kellan asked Zoe to bring me dinner, and he only came back later after having his martial arts practice. We went to bed in silence, and I was trying so hard to keep my tears from falling.

I thought that he would slowly let me in. I thought that I could be closer to him and understand him better. But just as I thought that he had broken down his walls, he returned to the way he'd been before.

It pains me to know how much he's been suffering. The closer I get to him, the more I can feel his pain and the more I can feel the man behind that cold exterior.

His words hurt, but I know that it's just a camouflage to hide his pain. I've promised myself that I will make him see the good things in life, that he can still be happy despite his disability, and that he's worth it.

After I finish drying my hair, I plop myself on the bed. While I'm wondering what I'm about to do today, someone knocks on the door.

I open it and find Zoe standing before me with a warm smile on her face.

She doesn't have any tray of food with her, so I wonder what her plan is. Spending a day with her is exactly what I need right now, and so my heart is filled with relief.

"Morning," I greet her with a cheerful smile. "Are we going to have breakfast together?"

I don't know if Luca and his friends will be around to harass me again, but having a friend with me is better than being alone. My heart hurts as I remember that Kellan reminded me to stay out of his way.

Zoe nods, and we happily hook each other's arms, walking down the hallway.

But then, instead of going to the kitchen, Zoe leads me to the basement. I raise my eyebrows in question, and she just signals with her hand that it's going to be okay.

It's not the same basement where they have the boxing ring, so I guess that it's the one where Zoe and her father live.

She pushes the door open, and I'm greeted by a tattoo studio.

I travel my eyes around with awe. The room is dimlit, but I can clearly see how artistic it is. The walls are lined up with dark paintings, and most of the furniture is dark wood. But strangely, it still feels comfortable enough for a living space. It even feels cozy.

I see two doors leading to different bedrooms and another door that I guess would lead to the bathroom. Just when I land my gaze on it, someone opens it from the other side.

I watch as a tall and broad-shouldered middle-aged man walks to us with a big smile on his face.

"You must be Layla." He reaches out his arm and gives me a firm handshake. "I'm Stas, Zoe's father. Welcome to our home."

I return his smile, appreciating his warm hospitality. This humble man has inked countless tattoos for the leaders and members of Black Wings.

"You're finally going to have your first tattoo, aren't you?" His question startles me, and as soon as he sees the panic on my face, he laughs. "Don't worry. It won't hurt that much. Do you want me to do it for you? Or do you want Zoe to do it? It's your choice."

I snap my head toward Zoe, who bites her lip uneasily and scratches her temple. She takes out a note from her pocket and writes to me.

I'm sorry. I know that you might not want it, but today is the day you'll get your tattoo. Kellan said so. It's an order.

My eyes widen in shock. I don't think that I'll ever be ready for a tattoo. I've heard that it's going to hurt, and I'm not planning to get my skin inked.

Zoe sighs.

This is a way for you to be completely safe here. Everybody knows the rules, and now you're the only exception.

One day, someone may take advantage of Kellan's disability and hurt you. Non-members are not supposed to be here. Outsiders have been killed in this place.

I gasp at that information, slapping my hands over my mouth.

There are people with grudges in here, people who wouldn't tolerate such unfairness. I really don't want to risk you getting hurt.

I have no choice but to admit my defeat. If it's the only way for me to survive this place, I'll do it.

I just never thought that I would be a member of a mafia or gangster family kind of thing.

Zoe's eyes soften as she notices my willingness to proceed with the tattoo.

"All settled?" Stas' voice breaks the silence.

I almost forgot that he's here.

He watches us with amusement before excusing himself. "I guess you trust Zoe more. Go have your girls' time. I'll be leaving," he jokes, giving me a pat on my shoulder.

I watch as he pushes through the door and steps out of the tattoo studio.

"Your dad seems fun and cool," I say to Zoe, and she only shrugs.

She hands me another note.

Are you ready?

I swallow and nod. I guess that I have no other choices.

Getting inked is definitely an experience that I won't forget for the rest of my life, but it's not as horrible as I thought it would be.

There are tears and little screams, of course, but it's not that bad. Thanks to Zoe, who makes me feel like I'm getting tattooed by an angel. She's constantly trying to calm me down with her gestures. She handles me with gentleness and care -- she even stops and hugs me a few times during the process.

By the time Zoe finishes the tattoo, Stas comes back with a set of new tools. The moment his eyes land on my tattoo, which is inked on the back of my right shoulder, his eyes widen.

"Is that really the one that he instructed you to do for her?" His voice is filled with disbelief.

Uneasiness stirs inside me. I can't imagine if this is the wrong tattoo and I have to go through it one more time.

Positive.

Zoe responds to her father with sign language.

I learned sign language before I applied for the care agency to anticipate possible requirements from potential clients, but I wasn't an expert at it because I only had little time to learn about it.

Zoe doesn't know that I can read sign language, and that's why she's been communicating with me through notes. Now that I see her doing it, I can vaguely guess what she's trying to say.

Yes. It's the one he ordered me to make for her when he came to see me this morning. There was no way that I misheard him.

"What?" Worry fills my tone. "What's happening? What's wrong with my tattoo?"

I can't see it yet because it's inked on the back of my shoulder. They go silent for a while before Stas finally sighs.

"Well, Layla..." He sounds like it's difficult for him to explain, and I don't like the way his voice shakes.

What could possibly make him slightly nervous? I bet that he's made thousands of tattoos, so what could be wrong with this one that he couldn't even find words to explain it?

"I don't think we have the capacity to tell you about this tattoo," he says. "Only Kellan knows the reasons for it. You can just ask him when you meet him again."

My worry escalates. I turn my head toward Zoe, who gives me the same guilty look.

"I'm sorry, Layla," Stas speaks again. "We can't give you the answer. We don't want to surpass Kellan's authority."

I feel like I'm about to cry. Now that I think about it, the last time I saw Kellan he was freaking mad at me.

Maybe he gave me this tattoo to punish me, not to protect me.

"You did the best you could," Stas says to Zoe, ruffling her hair. He gives her a kiss on the forehead. "I'm so proud of you."

Zoe smiles with tears brimming in her eyes, and I don't even know whether it's a sad smile or a happy one.

"I think it's better to wait for Kellan to announce it himself. I don't think that anyone would be ready for this." Stas straightens up.

Zoe quickly nods and hurriedly helps me wear my clothes back to cover my tattoo.

"Go with her for breakfast," Stas says to his daughter.

My heart is beating like a drum in my chest.

"Don't worry, Layla," Stas says while Zoe and I are heading to the door.

I glance back at him, only to find him looking at me with a serious expression.

"Everything will be all right."

That's the last thing I hear before Zoe drags me out of their home.

16

CHAPTER 16

LAYLA

Zoe and I make our way to the kitchen. She only gives me silence and an apologetic look when I ask her about the tattoo again along the way.

"Please, I need to know what will happen to me." I halt as we almost reach the kitchen.

She shakes her head, and my heart sinks with disappointment again. She places her palm over my heart and gives me a reassuring smile, as if she's trying to tell me that everything will be okay. But it's not enough for me.

Someone bumps into me, and when I look at the person, I see Nina, the girl whom I met when I first stepped into this mansion.

"If it isn't the girl without the tattoo." She sneers and then tosses Zoe a degrading look. "You've got yourself a friend, Layla. A stupid mute."

My heart burns with anger after hearing how she spoke about Zoe.

"Just leave us alone," I bite out.

"Layla," someone booms, and the entire room's attention is immediately on me.

Shivers run down my spine as I spot Luca walking toward me with his two friends. One of them indeed resembles Marco, and I snap my head around to find the other brother, hoping that he will show up and knock some sense into them again.

"I think it's about time that Kellan trashes you." Luca stops in front of me while everyone else goes silent. "He hasn't said any warning again after the first one, and as far as I can see, you're the one who's always on his tail."

"Do you not have anything else to do other than bullying someone?" I speak through gritted teeth. "An important mission, perhaps?"

Luca clenches his jaw, and I know that I just hit the right spot. His ego is bruised.

"Watch your tongue," he snaps, advancing toward me.

Zoe steps in front of me, shielding me from him.

Luca chuckles, eyeing her with pity. "Step away, you fucking mute. Don't interfere with my business with her. It's about time that she knows who's in charge here."

Zoe shakes her head firmly. When Luca takes one more step forward, she daringly pushes his chest, earning gasps from the people around us. It's not every day that we see an innocent, mute girl picking a fight with one of the Knights' right-hand man.

Rage takes over Luca, and before I know it, he pushes her with such force that she hits a table around the corner. My eyes widen in horror as I watch her fall onto the floor.

"What the hell did you just do to her?" I shout angrily at Luca before rushing to help her.

Zoe winces in pain. She takes my hand when I help her up.

"Are you okay?" I ask, worry laced in every word.

She nods. My anger builds up as I see the bruise on her forehead.

"Are you crazy?" Marco's brother shouts in Luca's face while his own face suddenly turns white as a paper. "Cole will be pissed if he knows about this."

"Shut up," Luca barks.

I frown in confusion. In the back of my mind, I sense something between Zoe and Cole, but I can't be sure.

"Important mission, you said?" Luca scoffs at me.

I automatically retreat as he steps closer to me and Zoe.

"Do you even have any idea where the men who went on such a mission are now?" He takes another threatening step. "Did they even succeed? That's bullshit. Fenrir told me that he couldn't even contact them anymore. They've been missing for days."

Zoe's face pales, and her eyes are now glistening with tears. The mute girl who just held her head up high despite being harassed is now close to crying.

"You're worried about Cole?" Luca hisses to Zoe, his voice full of hatred. "You should."

I can't help but think about my phone call with Jaxon, which ended abruptly because of gunshots and explosions. Until today, I haven't heard from him again, not even a reply to my text message.

Indeed, something really bad has happened to Jaxon, Cole, and Levi. But I refuse to believe that they're dead.

"And you." Luca glares at me. "You might be Kellan's slave, but a rule is a rule. The punishment is death if someone steps into our base without being a part of us. Kellan wouldn't know the truth because he's fucking blind. He can't even see your tattoo."

I tilt my chin up defiantly, but then he grips it harshly to the point that it hurts.

"Don't tell me that you've been manipulating him all this time." His voice is as cold as ice. "Because if that's the case, I'm sure that he won't mind if we use you and kill you afterward."

I'm trying to break free, but his friend holds me back, securing both of my wrists against my back. I glance at Zoe, only to find her being held back by Marco's brother. Her eyes widen in fear. She's afraid of what Luca will do to me.

"Too bad, isn't it?" Luca smirks, staring down at me with a look that makes me nauseous. "Kellan can't see this beauty. I'm sure that he won't mind if we replace you with another slave. There will be no difference for him, right?" He then laughs out loud.

My eyes burn with angry tears. "Let me go."

I scream as Luca snatches a knife from the kitchen table and grips my t-shirt collar to the point that it almost chokes me and causes my feet to leave the ground.

He aims the knife at my shirt, the tip touching the soft fabric. "No. Let everyone witness the lies you've been feeding him."

My heart almost stops as I feel the sharp blade against my skin. He's going to rip my shirt off in front of everybody.

"You're just a girl without the tattoo. Filthy little liar. Fucking intruder."

It's too late. I can't prevent it.

My body is shaking with fear when Luca tears my shirt with the knife. The torn fabric falls to the floor, leaving me standing here topless, only in my bra.

Gasps and frantic murmurs fill the air. The guy locking my wrist suddenly releases me, making me stumble forward and almost crash into Luca's chest.

Strangely, Luca steps backward. His eyes are not focused on me but on his friend behind me instead. I look over my shoulder and find him looking at my back with pure horror.

"What the fuck is that?" His voice is shaking uncontrollably.

I snap my head around, only to find people staring at me with the same fear in their eyes.

There's a mirror hanging on the wall across me, so I take a peak, praying to God that this won't be the end of me. My heart is thumping widely against my ribcage.

The moment I see my tattoo, inked on the back of my shoulder, time seems to stop.

I see a pair of black wings. It's not big, just enough to cover the right side on the back of my shoulder. It's beautiful, made by Zoe. I almost can't believe that such beauty is now permanently etched on my skin.

But it's not only that. I can see now why they are all staring at it in shock. It's not a regular black wings tattoo -- it has gold streaks on it.

I haven't seen anyone among Black Wings members wearing this kind of tattoo. I also remember Nina explaining to me that the streaks are either silver or red.

"Impossible." Luca's voice is also shaking. His eyes are glued to my tattoo, which is now facing him.

People are whispering and talking more frantically. They're trying to gauge what it is.

"You can't have that kind of tattoo," Luca echoes in disbelief. "It's not possible."

"What do you think we're seeing now?" a random girl shouts madly at him. "You're doomed. You're going to be dead."

"Yeah," another one shouts. This time, it's a guy's voice. "We shouldn't be doing this to her. You just dug all of our graves."

My head pulses with pain, and it feels like the room is spinning. I don't understand what's happening.The people around me start to argue with one another, talking loudly and angrily.

Panic fills the air, and everything becomes chaos. The words tossed around me and the history of Black Wings that I have learned before are playing in my head.

Different kinds of Black Wings tattoos represent the identity of the person.

Black -- regular members.

Black with red streaks -- the Knights, considered the leaders of Black Wings. As of now, there are three of them -- Cole, Levi, and Fenrir.

Black with silver streaks -- the Kings. This kind of tattoo belongs to the owner of Black Wings and all of his heirs sharing the same blood. Jaxon and Kellan have it. Should their sister still live in this world, she would have the same tattoo.

Then there's another one, the kind of tattoo they rarely talk about because they have never seen one.

Black with gold streaks. This tattoo belongs to a person of importance who isn't related by blood to the family. They are no less important than the Kings and to be protected at all costs. There's only one person who got this tattoo before, and it was Jaxon's and Kellan's mother. Her tattoo was gifted by her husband.

I grip the table on my side for support, listening to the crowd going crazy around me.

"Is that really true?" someone shouts. "What the hell is that tattoo supposed to mean?"

"Mine," a voice answers firmly, and everyone instantly turns quiet.

Goosebumps crawl on my skin. When I turn around to see the person to whom the voice belongs, my heart freezes in place.

Kellan has entered the room. He's wearing a jacket, looking like he just came back from his morning jog. The deadly look on his face is enough to make anyone cower under it.

"It means that she's fucking mine," he says in a threatening voice.

I know that he's doing this to protect me, but his expression and the way he said that makes me wonder if he really means it. Whatever it is, huge relief washes over me, and I can't help the tears pooling in my eyes.

"No one touches Layla," he commands, making the silence that goes by even worse. It's like everyone doesn't even dare move a finger when he speaks. "I repeat," he hisses venomously. "No one. No one can fucking touch her."

His anger is consuming him as a whole. I can see his body shaking with rage, and that sight is enough to make me run to him.

He catches me in his arms, and I immediately bury my face in his chest, letting my tears fall freely.

I don't care. I can't contain this relief inside me.

A soft smile touches my lips when he tightens his hold on me.

17

CHAPTER 17

L AYLA

More weeks have passed since Kellan gave me the tattoo, and things have changed significantly inside the mansion.

No one dares to bully me anymore although I can still feel their gazes at me. Luca and his friends magically disappear from my sight. Rumors say that Fenrir has heard about the incident happening in the kitchen and that now Luca and his friends are on a mission with only a 10% chance of survival. I wonder if it's some kind of punishment for them.

People still whisper about me behind my back. I know that they can't believe what's happening, that I -- out of all the members of Black Wings -- got the tattoo colored in black with gold streaks. Giving me a regular tattoo would be enough to protect me here, so I also wonder why Kellan had me inked with that tattoo.

After having my lunch with Zoe at her place, I step back into Kellan's room, only to find him standing near the window with his back facing the door. The moment he hears me coming in, he turns around, accidentally knocking one of the photo frames on his desk.

I'm about to help him pick it up when he reaches for it. I look at the photo, the one of him when he was still a little boy, sitting side by side with a little girl. She's smiling sweetly while he has a smirk on his face. I have guessed that it's his younger sister, who died in the car accident.

"Is that..." I falter as he puts the frame back on the desk. "Your sister?" I ask, feeling that my heart is beating faster.

Things have been good between us nowadays, and I'm afraid that my question will trigger him. It's not easy to be close to Kellan because he's been putting up his walls for years. Speaking about his sister may cause him to draw back again, but I'm just so curious. I want him to tell me more about him and his family.

His lips twitch in irritation as sudden pain crosses his expression.

"I'm sorry," I quickly say. "I didn't mean to... I didn't mean to make you remember the pain of losing her. I just wanted to ask. She's beautiful."

Kellan doesn't respond. He walks toward the bed and sits on it. Since I've been living with him, I've learned the way he reacts when he's trying to shut off. He's restless now, and it's one of the signs. Then he will become angry and lets it out to the people around him. His trauma makes him easily get enraged every time he remembers the pain.

But I know that he can become better. We still fight, but it's more like bickering now, definitely not as bad as before, and definitely less frequent.

I sit on the bed beside him and whisper, "I'm sorry."

I'm sure that he can hear my pain too.

"I'm so sorry that you lost her."

He swallows.

Seconds pass in silence, but then he opens his mouth. "At first, I couldn't believe that she was gone." His voice is filled with agony, and it breaks my heart. "I protected her with my life. I was sure that I engulfed her so that nothing could hurt her, not even when I felt extreme pain all over my body. The last thing I felt against my chest before I blacked out was her heartbeat. She couldn't be gone."

Now I'm not even sure that I can hear their story. It's too painful.

"Kellan," I breathe, not wanting him to continue the story if he can't. But on the other hand, another part of me wants him to let it out so that the anger wouldn't suffocate him.

"I don't fucking know why, but a part of me insists that she's still alive, living somewhere, breathing," he says, his intense gray eyes darkening.

He sounds like he still has much more to say, but then his face falls. There's nothing but sorrow in his expression.

"Even if she were still alive, I might not be able to recognize her anymore. My fucking eyes..."

My heart almost stops as I hear that sentence from him. Instinctively, I reach out for his hand to comfort him, but the moment our fingers graze each other, he pulls away like my touch is fire.

Soon, he's panting and drawing away from me.

I immediately regret what I did. I was going too far. Even though it was just a little touch of comfort, Kellan wasn't ready for that.

K E L L AN

Even though I can't see her, I know that my reaction hurts her. I can hear the sound of her shaky breath after I snap her hand off.

I want to shut off. I'm not ready for her warmth. I hate the way she makes me feel vulnerable. I hate the way she's trying hard to cut my heart and see what's inside it.

I feel her moving from my bed, and it makes me ball my fist. Damn. Now that she's leaving, I don't know how to make things right. I wait for her to step out of my room, but to my surprise, the sound of her footsteps gives me a sign that she's walking in the other direction.

"Can I turn on the music player?" she asks.

I don't know what to say. I'm not against it, and I think she knows anyway because the next thing I hear is the sound of music from my vinyl record player.

Melody of classic ballads echoes in my room, and my heart sinks. It's been ages since I turned on this music player. I usually listen to music from my phone using my headset when I find it hard to fall asleep, so when this song is playing from my vinyl record, I can't help but remember the last time it played in my room.

It was when I did what my therapist suggested a year after my parents' death. He told me to grieve the loss of my parents, to let out the pent-up emotions for good. The song used to be the one my parents played when they danced together.

The last time I heard it in this very same room, I was sobbing uncontrollably. I was 12 back then.

It's amazing that the music player is still functioning right now.

Layla hums softly. "I think I know this song," she mumbles. "Yeah. I think this song was playing when I was practicing slow dancing in my school."

Dancing.

My mind wanders to the time Layla asked me to dance in the rain, and I badly want her to feel like that again, especially after I just denied her a few moments ago.

I don't know whether it's just my guilt or the fact that I need the sound of her laughter again.

"Do you want to do it?" I blurt.

She doesn't say anything back.

Of course, she doesn't. She won't understand what I'm trying to say if I don't make it clear. I suddenly feel fucking stupid.

"Dancing," I say. "Do you want to dance to the music now?"

After a while, Layla laughs softly. "Only if you dance with me," she says with a slight teasing tone. "The dance is for two people, anyway."

I don't say anything, but I bet she can see that I'm not objecting to it.

"Come here," she says in a cheerful voice.

I reluctantly stand up. I don't know what I just fucking said. I can't fucking dance, and this is going to be fucking embarrassing.

"Come on. It's okay. I won't bite," she teases again, earning my scowl, which only makes her laugh.

My pulse quickens as she takes my hand. She places her other hand on my shoulder.

"Have you ever done this?" she asks.

"You think?" I ask menacingly.

"I was just asking."

I can feel the movement of her arms when she shrugs.

"If that's the case, I'm going to teach you a bit," she says. "I'm not an expert, so I'm just going to tell you about the basic steps."

My lips form into a thin line. I might be acting indifferently in front of her, but I'm actually anxious.

I never stood this close to any other girl.

She's too close. I can smell her addicting scent even better, and I can feel the warmth of her body against mine like it's a part of me. Her hands feel so small compared to mine -- it's either mine are too big or hers are the size of a little girl's.

"Okay, now I'm going to step to your right, and you just have to follow me." She does as she says, and I follow her.

Yet, I can't focus because of the overwhelming closeness between us. I feel like burning under her fingertips, and her sweet scent makes me feel like I'm breathing heroin.

"Again," she says.

I almost stumble because I can't concentrate.

"Easy," she says. "We're going to do this slowly. Now, to your left." She repeats the steps, but I'm still struggling to follow her.

After a few more minutes, we can finally find our rhythm although I still make a few mistakes here and there.

It's silly that I can master martial arts like a pro but I can't even do these simple steps. She's distracting me.

When the song changes, Layla finally stops. "Okay. You're not that bad."

I squint at her.

"Okay, you're actually terrible." She giggles, and her sweet laughter sips into my soul like a drug I am forced to take.

I don't even know whether she's a drug or a poison, but it's one that I don't mind taking.

What the fuck am I thinking about?

"Read," I say out of the blue.

She must be confused because she doesn't say anything again.

"Excuse me?" she echoes.

"Read," I repeat. "You once asked me if I read anything. I read books. I want to do that now."

"Oh, sure," she quickly says, sounding embarrassed that she just figured it out.

She pulls away, and the loss of her warmth is already making my heart long for it.

I walk toward the recliner sofa and sit on it. Layla follows me and stops beside the bookshelf.

"Which books do you want to read?" she asks.

"Not the braille books. I've read them all," I say. "I want to read something else."

She turns silent, giving me the impression that she's a little lost.

"Can you read it for me?" I ask, surprised that I can speak so nicely. I usually order people around and command them, making them cower under my authority.

This girl is changing me. I don't think that she knows the extent of her effect on me.

"Sure," Layla says.

I let out a sigh of relief. It's crazy how I feel anxious just because I need someone to do something simple like this.

I just need to keep hearing her voice -- that's why I asked her to read to me -- but she doesn't have to know it.

When we first met, I thought that her voice was annoying, but it was only because it affected me.

"Which book do you want me to read to you?" Layla asks.

I feel stupid because I don't even think about it. I just want her to read something to me.

My little sister, Inez, used to lend me her favorite books. I haven't read them again for a long time because they're not braille books.

"It's somewhere on the shelf next to my desk," I say. "They are regular books. Just pick the one you're interested in. They're the best ones."

They really are because I'm not going to insult Inez's treasures. I still remember the excitement on Inez's face and how she spoke giddily every time she just found a new favorite.

She always forced me to read it too, and I gladly accepted it.

"What about this?" Layla echoes, sounding like she's reading the title of the book she just picked from the shelf. "Milk and honey?"

It's a poetry book written by Inez's favorite Indian-Canadian poet Rupi Kaur. Ironically, it's the last book Inez lent to me before she died.

"I guess it's a yes?" Layla says, and I can imagine her raising her eyebrows. "You're not frowning nor scowling. It's a yes," she teases.

I roll my eyes, but I don't feel annoyed, strangely. She moves the chair behind the desk closer to me so that she can sit in front of me. I hear the sound of her flipping the pages.

"Shall we begin?" she asks.

I nod.

Slowly, she reads it to me, "The night after you left, I woke up so broken. The only place to put the pieces were the bags under my eyes."

I breathe, listening to her soothing voice. It's soft, calming me. The weight of the sentence doesn't bother me.

"I am hopelessly a lover and a dreamer and that will be the death of me." More words leave her mouth.

I feel like I can listen to her forever. I realize that it's not only her laughter that I like to hear but also every sound she makes. Even the sound of her whisper at the end of the sentence does something to me, and I don't know how she does that.

The only sound that I hate to hear from her is the sound of her crying. At first, I thought that it was just irritating. But now, the thought of hearing her cries makes me livid.

Layla reads the book so smoothly like flowing water -- I don't even remember the time passing while I'm listening to her. I don't know how long we've been staying like this -- me sitting here while listening to her voice and her reading the books to me with so much gentleness.

"Fall in love..." she begins again, and I open my mouth too.

"With your solitude," we say in unison.

I remember those words because I think about them countless times, every time I feel lonely.

"The way--"

"What color?" I interrupt in the middle of her sentence -- the words slip from my tongue.

"Sorry?" she asks in confusion.

"Your hair."

Silence falls, and I bet that she doesn't understand why the hell I'm asking such a question.

"Um, auburn," she says.

I nod, contrary to the turmoil in my mind. It's such a simple answer for anyone else, but it's not an easy one for me.

I hear her flipping the pages again, but before she can continue reading the book to me, I ask her again, "What about your eyes?"

She turns silent again, and I continue, "What color are they?"

"They're blue," she says. "Why are you suddenly asking me these questions?"

A frown touches my lips. "Just wondering."

When she starts reading the words again, I can no longer hear what she says. These questions are still stuck in my head, and restlessness begins to consume me.

My heart is beating faster, and soon, I'm going to be consumed in anger. I can already feel my body shaking.

Goddammit.

I abruptly stand up, earning a soft gasp from her.

"What's wrong?" she asks in concern.

But I have to go. I need to find the answers, and I can't stay here. I'm angry, and I will only hurt her feelings.

"Kellan," her voice rings in my ears as I storm out of my room. I slam the door shut behind me with so much force, I almost think that I broke the hinge.

I skip a few steps while I'm running down the stairs. I put my weight onto the railing so I can jump. I don't even fucking care if I fall.

Once I reach the back door, I storm through it, heading toward the backyard. I make my way through the path leading to a small forest at the back of the property like a madman. I think I'm going to be crazy.

The sound of my foot stepping on a twig on the grass is so loud, it rings in my ears. The three branches prick my skin while I'm forcing my way through the forest, and it feels painful, I'm almost sure that it makes me bleed.

I'm so sensitive to touch. I can even feel the afternoon rays from the sun burning my face.

I almost walk into a tree, so I punch my fist into it, making my knuckles crack. The birds above me fly frantically, making sounds like the chaos in my head.

The smell of the leaves strikes my nostrils, I can almost taste it in my mouth.

I can feel everything.

I can hear everything.

Hell, I can even hear the wind whispering to me.

But I can't fucking see.

My knees drop to the ground. I dig the soil with my bare hands, gritting my teeth. The soil... It's the closest thing I can find with the same color as her hair. Maybe it's not even the same -- I don't fucking know.

The soil escapes my palm while I'm trying to grip it. I can smell it. I can feel every drop of it tickling my skin, and I may even taste it if I have to, but I can't remember the color of it.

I pant, dropping my back onto the ground as I stare up at the sky with my arms spread wide. I'm facing the sky, and I know that it's blue, but I can't remember the color of blue anymore.

What color is blue?

What color are her eyes?

"Fuck," I curse, trying to control my heavy breathing.

I never wanted to see again so badly like this.

I want to see her eyes.

Her smile.

Her hair.

I want to see everything about her.

I squeeze my eyes shut and roll onto my side, feeling the breeze blowing through me, as though it wants to take my pain away with it. But it can't.

Goddammit, it hurts. It fucking hurts.

I want to see Layla, the girl who has the guts to make her way into my heart.

I want to stare into her eyes when she speaks to me.

I want to watch her beautiful smile curve on her lips when I amuse her.

I even want to see her angry face.

But there's only one thing my eyes can see.

Darkness.

18

— ◦ —

CHAPTER 18

LAYLA

While I'm walking toward the kitchen to refill the jug of water for Kellan, my mind goes back to what happened with him yesterday. I feel like I almost got through him. He's slowly letting me in, and I want nothing else but to see the real caring, unselfish man within him.

The intensity I felt when we danced keeps coming back into my mind too.

I might have tried to hide it with my cheerful attitude, but my heart was actually beating really fast every time I was close to him.

Behind that cold exterior, I can see the person he really is.

The man with such protective traits for the people dear to him.

The man who was willing to sacrifice himself to protect his little sister, so much so that his sight was taken away from him when he was trying to save her.

The man who is consistently angry because he can't do anything to help his brother.

After I fill the jug with water in the kitchen, I turn around the corner and bump into some guy's chest.

I almost scream as he covers my mouth in his hand. The jug of water falls from my hands, the glass shattering into pieces on the ground. He drags me towards another hallway, a deserted one, and corners me against the wall.

My eyes widen as I see Marco staring down at me. He signals with his finger over his mouth to keep me quiet. I don't know what he's going to do, but the only thing I can do is nod so that he can release me. His eyes soften, and slowly, he lets go of his hand.

"What are you doing?" I ask.

Nobody would do something like that to me again after knowing my tattoo, but on the other hand, I know that Marco is a nice guy. I don't think that he's going to hurt me.

"I left for weeks because they gave me a very lame job, and now that I'm back, all I can hear is everyone talking about you and Kellan," he says, sounding pissed. "Is that true?"

"Do you know about my tattoo?" I ask him back.

He nods. "I know. That's ridiculous."

I frown. That's not the reaction I expected. The other members fear it.

"Did he think he could just claim you with a tattoo? With that kind of bullshit?" he raises his voice, his anger becoming more visible in his expression.

"I don't think he did," I say. "He was only trying to protect me."

Disbelief skates on Marco's face. His eyes widen in shock. "What has he done to you? Did you even hear yourself? Don't you remember what kind of person he is? He's a horrible person."

I'm surprised by how offended I am after hearing that statement from Marco.

"I've been living with him, and I think I've gotten to know him better," I say. "He's been through a lot. We can't judge his feelings unless we have gone through a similar experience. I'm trying to help him heal."

"What the fuck does that mean?" Marcos snaps, and I'm surprised to hear him speaking in such anger. He literally looks like he's about to explode.

"Look, Layla." He grabs my shoulders, startling me. "I know you. I see myself when I see you. You're not supposed to be here, Layla. And we're not supposed to turn ourselves into those kinds of people. We're better than them."

I remember Marco's story that he was only trying to find his brother, which made him stuck in this world. I still have my respect for him because he didn't let his brother and Luca bully me.

"Kellan is a king here." It's impossible to not recognize his hatred when he speaks of Kellan. "But his heart is rotten. In fact, he has none."

"You don't know his heart," I say firmly. "No one here is trying to understand him because of the walls he built around him. He's blind. He has no sight. How do you expect him to know everything and control everything around here? And his brother might be dying on a mission. Give him a break, Marco."

The shock on his face is even more palpable now. "I can't believe I just heard that. The way you spoke of him, it was as if..." He's at a loss for words. "You can't be too close to him. He'll corrupt you."

My lips form into a thin line. I don't like the way Marco speaks of Kellan. Why does he hate Kellan so much?

"I thought we were the same," Marco hisses in frustration. "I thought neither of us wanted to be a part of Black Wings, but then as soon as you got that tattoo--"

"It's not about my tattoo," I finally snap at him.

He grips my shoulders harder, it hurts.

"Marco," I hiss in pain.

"So, the rumor is true," Marco speaks through gritted teeth. "Are you really with him? You can't be with a guy like him. He can't see you, Layla. He can't even see your beauty. He won't appreciate you. He won't be able to make you happy."

"What's that supposed to mean?" I ask, hurt by his words.

He quickly swallows, realizing his mistake. "I didn't mean it like that. Please, Layla, listen to me."

I'm already struggling to get free from his hold when I notice movement from the corner of my eye. I snap my head and find Zoe staring at us with wide eyes. Panic and worry immediately cross her expression.

Marco glances at her and curses. "Shit." He returns his gaze to me and says firmly, "We're not done. We'll talk again later." With that said, he finally releases me and strides toward the end of the hallway.

I place my palm over my heart, trying to calm my racing heartbeat. Marco is the only Black Wings member that I think I can be friends with -- other than Zoe and her father. But after this incident, I don't know if I can see him indifferently. There's a huge disappointment in my heart because I might have just lost a friend.

Zoe rushes to me, checking my condition. There's only concern on her face.

"I'm okay," I say weakly.

I sigh as Zoe gives me a comforting hug.

More days pass.

I haven't seen Kellan all evening today, so I make my way down to the basement. It's about time that Kellan has his dinner. I wonder if he has lost track of time.

I push through the door and find him in the boxing ring. He's practicing alone. There's no one else here. The entire place would be deserted if it weren't because of us.

I step closer toward the ring, watching Kellan. He's doing his martial arts move so fast, like the wind, and so precise. It feels like I'm watching a beautiful art being played in front of me, just like the first time I saw him.

He's beautiful, just like his lonely soul. If only he could see it himself. If only he could let himself be happy again.

Kellan Romero is better than he thinks he is, better than most of the people spending their lives in this place.

It seems that he can feel my movement because he suddenly stops.

He turns his body in my direction. "Why didn't you wait in my room?"

A sigh leaves my lips. I smile. I don't answer him and walk closer instead.

He grabs the rope at the side of the ring and jumps out of it. I pick up his towel, which is lying at the corner of the ring, and meet him halfway.

"How did you know that it was me?" I ask in a curious tone.

He sighs. "Your footsteps. I know how you walk. I couldn't be mistaken."

I chuckle lightly. Instead of handing him the towel, I help him dry himself with it, starting by patting his face lightly before wiping his upper body gently.

He's full of sweat, but he can't be more beautiful. A blush creeps on my cheeks as the towel makes contact with his abs.

It seems that he notices my uneasiness because the next thing he does is guide my hands to wrap the towel around his shoulders. Shivers run down my spine as my fingers graze his bare skin in the process. I'm about to pull away and let go of the towel when he prevents me from doing so. He catches my wrists with both hands and secures my arms around his shoulders instead.

I don't know what to do in this awkward position, so I just pat the back of his shoulders lightly. I hope that he doesn't notice my hands slightly shaking because of this intimate position.

"I've been wanting to try something," he says, his voice hoarse.

My brows furrow in confusion. "What is it?" I whisper.

He swallows, and I can see that he's nervous too. The muscles on his neck move.

He touches my chin with two fingers, startling me. He squints, like he's thinking hard. My heart thumps as his thumb grazes my lower lip.

"Lips," he whispers.

My heart beats even faster. He's studying me and trying to memorize me in his mind.

"Lips," I repeat his word, my lips slightly trembling because of the emotions building up inside me.

I close my eyes and sigh. I can hear his shaky breath when he feels the air from my mouth blowing his thumb.

I feel his fingers move upward, touching my nose.

"Nose," he says, and I can't help the smile curving on my lips.

"Nose," I whisper.

I open my eyes because I want to see his expression. He's staring at me deeply.

When his thumbs reach the area under my tear ducts, he whispers again, "Eyes."

There's no way that I can't hear the pain in his voice. He sounds like he's in agony.

His grey eyes turn glassy. I'm staring into them, and he's staring into mine, but it's only me who can see.

His eyes are the most enchanting and captivating grey. I can stare into them forever and get drowned in them. Grey is my favorite color now. There's no doubt as I think about that.

My vision starts to get blurry with tears. "Eyes." I nod, and that's when a tear drops, falling onto his finger.

It startles him. "Don't cry," he says, wiping away my tear.

I tighten my grip on his shoulders to compose myself, causing his face to draw closer to mine. We're aware of how dangerously close we are to each other, but none of us are able to pull back.

"Layla, may I..." He stops mid-sentence, sounding like it pains him to utter the next words.

My heart is racing inside my chest. He may what?

"May I kiss your lips?" he asks softly.

The butterflies inside my tummy go crazy. I swallow. "Yes." My voice is so small, but I'm sure that he can hear it.

I can't believe that I just said that.

He clears his throat. "I may be bad at it. I haven't done it before."

"I haven't done it either," I say truthfully.

Never had I thought that I would have my first kiss with Kellan Romero.

I can't figure out what he feels about my confession. The more I'm trying to figure out what he's thinking in his mind, the more I'm becoming crazy.

Kellan looks extremely nervous too. His face hardens, and I close my eyes. The next thing I feel is his nose touching mine.

I snap my eyes open and suddenly blurt, "Wait."

He immediately holds back.

"If you're worried about what the girl you're going to kiss for the first time looks like, you don't need to think about it at all." I'm blabbering like a mess because of how nervous I am. "Just believe that you're about to kiss the prettiest girl on the planet."

What the hell am I talking about? I instantly regret what I said, but it's too late.

To my amazement, Kellan chuckles softly. My eyes widen. It's the first time I see a smile on his face, and nothing could top what I'm feeling inside.

"My God." I breathe. "You just smiled," I say it like I couldn't believe my eyes.

It's the first time I saw it.

Kellan looks taken aback too, but then his eyes light up. The light in his eyes -- his happiness -- is a sight I want to memorize for the rest of my life.

"That's a good thing, isn't it?" The corner of his mouth crooks up in amusement. "I don't think that I ever did it for the past nine years."

His words make my heart swell, and I can only close my eyes when he leans in, brushing his lips against mine.

Our first kiss is tentative. Exploring. Like the first taste of freedom.

"Your lips are so soft." His voice is shaking as he whispers against my mouth.

Kellan is talking like the feeling is too overwhelming for him, but what he should know is that I feel the same thing.

I kiss him back with all my heart. We keep returning each other's kisses for a long minute, until he pulls away. My stomach churns. I'm afraid that he doesn't like it enough.

But then, when I open my eyes, I have the answer as to why he suddenly stopped.

"I'm so sorry for denying you." He clenches his jaw.

My chest tightens due to my feelings for him as he gives me another round of kisses.

19

CHAPTER 19

KELLAN

Layla Hayes is my undoing.

The thought rings in my head over and over again. It doesn't leave my mind, not when I have to train my fighters the day after Layla and I had our first kiss.

I'm now standing in the boxing ring again, but tonight, the basement is filled with people. The crowds roar, shout, and talk madly.

People are watching me fighting with the chosen members of Black Wings. I can hear some of them placing their bets on who's going to beat me. The ones who did place that stupid bet must be new because anyone else must have seen that no one has ever beaten me in a one-on-one fight.

My chest rises and falls as I wait for the next challenger. The crowd goes louder as I feel the person climbing up the ring. I take a large gulp of water from my water bottle and face him.

I catch the sound of his breath and the weight of his feet touching the ground. This one doesn't feel like a huge or bulky one, but he doesn't feel small either. He's average, but he definitely has a temper because he's panting in rage.

His nostrils flare like a bull, and I don't know why he's like that. It's usually the other way around when it comes to fighting with me. I'm usually the angry one.

Yet, after the kiss with Layla yesterday, I don't think that anything can make my mood sour. Goddammit, I can still taste her lips on mine, and the feeling of heaven is still very much in my mind.

I'd never felt that kind of happiness for such a long time.

But then, it also feels so overwhelming that I can't help but fear that when I wake up it will only be just a dream.

A guy shouts to indicate the start of the battle, and just as I expected, my opponent storms at me like a madman. His movement is fast, but I'm faster -- the result of my never-ending practices all over the years. Martial arts is my therapy, and my other senses are five times better than a normal person, so anyone who picked a fight with me would be a fool if they thought that they could beat me.

I duck his attack just when his fist is about to make contact with the side of my head. I use that split second of his imbalance to get low and kick his feet, making him fall with a loud thud on the ground.

The crowd roars, and I hear a guy shouting a curse to my opponent. It's not unusual for the audience to go barbaric when they watch the fight. They enjoy the violence, and sometimes their emotions take over.

I'm just glad that Layla isn't here to watch the fight. I don't like the idea of her standing among the crowd. It's not only the fight that is brutal but also the audience.

Honestly, I don't like the whole idea of her being here in Black Wings, no matter how much her existence makes me crave her emotionally like an addict. Layla and danger are not supposed to be in the same place.

The guy gets up after I kick him down. I know from his breath that he's getting even angrier. He storms at me again, and this time the tips of his fingers almost graze my neck. My adrenaline instantly rushes, and my eyes widen in shock. This guy is planning to choke me to death while pushing me against the rope at the side of the ring.

Before he can wrap his hands around my neck, I slip under his arm and get behind him. I kick his back so hard, he's thrown forward against the rope of the ring.

The crowd roars again as I pant in shock. Something is wrong with this. Something is fishy with this guy.

He attacked me like he wanted to kill me, literally kill me.

The force I used to kick him against the rope should have knocked him out, but instead, I am face to face with his wrath again. I can feel his piercing gaze on me when his body turns to me again, but I'm not going to give him any chance. I will fucking end this fight now.

It's actually good for their practice session that a member is being so persistent in defeating me, but my gut tells me that there's something wrong with this guy.

Before he can regain balance to storm at me again, I do it first. Our speed makes us meet each other halfway in the center of the ring, but since he's still unstable from my attack, he's not fast enough to dodge my punch into his face.

I hear a loud crack as his jaw breaks. The crowd cheers, almost making me deaf. My opponent falls again to the ground.

My jaw is clenched tightly, and my breathing is hard and fast.

To everyone's horror, he's still trying to get up. Loud gasps echo inside the basement, and I can even feel my heart rate kick up a notch.

He wants me down that badly, and I wonder who the fuck he is.

I lower myself to the ground to give him the final blow, but then the next thing I feel is pain stabbing my upper arm. I groan loudly while the crowd echoes loud gasps and curses.

He fucking stabbed me with a knife.

I hiss in pain. No one has ever stabbed me. I don't know what made him dare do it. Weapons are never allowed in every fight with me.

He could have stabbed me in my heart, but the position when I was about to give him the final blow -- with my thighs trapping the sides of his stomach and my arms caging him -- he could only aim the knife at the flesh of my arm.

"You deserve to die," he hisses. It's not only his voice that is shaking with rage but his entire body. "You should fucking die."

He still has his tight grip on the knife planted into my flesh. I let out a shaky breath when my hand hovers over his to grab the knife. I feel like I'm about to break his fingers when I finally wrap mine around the handle.

I grit my teeth, my body shaking with pain. With all the energy mustered in my body, I slowly pull out the knife, fighting his power to put it back into my flesh. My roar rings in the air as I stare up at the ceiling. The knife clatters on the base of the ring after I pull it out.

People are rushing into the ring to separate us. I hear him roar in anger while they are dragging him away from me.

"Stay away from her," he hollers.

My heart almost stops because I know who he's speaking about.

"Stay the fuck away from her," he continues snapping at me. "She's too good for you. You can't even protect her, and you'll never be able to, you fucking motherfucker."

He's seething, and it's chaos around us. It's at this very moment that I remember his voice. I've heard it before.

'Come on, man. You told her to get lost.'

He was the person shouting to me when I challenged my members near the fountain the night they were about to make Layla their slave.

"I defeated you," he roars. "I won. I got her. That was your promise. Now give her to me, you fucking asshole."

I pant, pressing the wound on my arm as I hear my own heaving breathing.

"Kellan, are you okay?" unfamiliar voices keep asking me when they rush to me.

This is the first time that a member has attacked a leader. I can imagine the shock on their faces.

"Please, hold on," someone says. "We'll get you checked by the doctor as soon as possible."

I squeeze my eyes shut, but it's not because of the pain.

Layla.

Why is she being dragged into this?

I can't stop thinking about his words.

She's too good for you.

You can't even protect her.

"What the fuck did you think you just do?" a panicked, hysterical voice fills the air, coming from my opponent's side. A guy is speaking to my opponent. "Fuck. Did you even know what you just did? Why did you attack Kellan?"

"Because he deserved it--"

"Marco," the guy warns him to stop, his voice filled with fear. Fear of the punishment and consequences that would happen after attacking me, their king.

Marco. It's not a familiar name to me. I don't think that I've ever spoken to him, so I fucking don't know why he could commit such an act.

My instinct tells me that he and Layla know each other. Judging from the way he spoke about her -- not to mention that he was already drawn to her at the night they were harassing her -- there's more to the story.

"Don't worry about it, Kellan." Someone crouches down next to me, snapping me out of my thoughts. "We'll make sure that he'll get the punishment he deserves."

There's only one punishment for betrayal, and it will be even worse because it's me -- their king -- that he just attacked.

Death. A painful death.

"No. Let him live." I grit my teeth.

I can imagine the surprise hitting the people surrounding me when I utter those words.

"Put him in our jail, and don't touch him until I fucking speak to him."

20

CHAPTER 20

KELLAN

Morning has arrived.

I let Layla clean my upper body with a damp cloth while I'm sitting inside the bathtub. The water reaches my hipbone, and I'm not fully naked. I'm still wearing my shorts.

She's helping me take a bath, and I'm so grateful for the way she treats the area near the wound with utmost care. Having her here calms me.

It's funny that I thought she annoyed the hell out of me at the beginning of our interactions. It was the denial speaking to me.

The doctor said that there was nothing to worry about my arm. The stab was not that deep – probably because Marco had lost so much energy after fighting me – and it wouldn't have any problem in healing.

I turn my head toward my upper arm, feeling Layla patting my shoulder blade gently. She tucks a strand of my wet hair that covers my eye, and I let out a shaky breath at the soft touch of her skin on my face.

"I can't believe that someone did this to you," she whispers.

She has said that countless times since last night, and I still haven't asked her about Marco.

I realize that I'm afraid of the answer. What if Marco is right?

I always knew that I couldn't protect her and that she would be too good to be true. That was why I kept denying her in the beginning. But then, refusing such an offer from heaven was proven too hard for a person who had been in enough hell like me, and so I just couldn't resist Layla.

"I wonder who did it," she mutters, sounding angry. "What a jerk. He cheated the fight. He wasn't supposed to use any weapon." She's talking as if she can't bear the thought of someone hurting me.

I keep my silence for a moment before I finally speak. "Marco. His name is Marco."

A gasp leaves her mouth, and it confirms my assumption that she knows him. Irritation builds up inside me, but I'm trying my best to compose myself.

"What?" she whispers in disbelief. Her hand touching my shoulder shakes, and she pulls away.

I can feel her sinking to the bathroom floor. She leans her head against the edge of the bathtub, and my fingers brush her hair gently.

"What happened?" I whisper, not wanting to make her even more upset than she is now. "Talk to me."

Layla breathes, and it's shaky. I hate it when she's hurt. I feel her straighten up and focus her attention on me again.

"I don't know. It's just--" She chokes, her voice laced with confusion. "I never thought that he would react like that. I should have made him understand better. Maybe I should have voiced my argument more properly. I should have talked to him again after I objected--"

"What do you mean?" Urgency is evident in my voice. I become restless, afraid that he might have done something terrible to her. "Did he force you to do something you didn't want? Did he hurt you?" I hiss venomously.

"No, it's not like that," Layla quickly says. "It's just..." She takes a deep breath, and the seconds that pass after that are so excruciating for me. "He actually cares about me, really cares. He's a good person, Kellan. He didn't harass or bully me like the other members did. He was shoved into Black Wings while he was only looking for his brother, and I feel like he's one of the few people here who truly understand how I feel. But lately, he became quite bold in getting what he wanted, especially after he went on his latest mission. I just--"

She lets out another shaky breath, sounding like she's about to cry. "I don't know what made him attack you like that. He shouldn't have done that. I feel bad for him because I know what kind of person he used to be, and I would be lying If I said I didn't care about him. But on the other hand, I'm livid that he attacked you. Oh, God." Her voice is shaking, and she sounds like she's covering her mouth with her hands. "If something even worse happened to you, I don't think," she stutters. "I don't think that I'll forgive--" She can't even continue her sentence.

I ball my fist tightly.

To say that I'm jealous would be an understatement. She's right. She can't hide the fact that she cares about him. But I get where she's coming from. At that time, he was the only man who managed to comfort her. I might have protected her in my own way, but I can't help but admit that my fucking mouth sometimes ruined everything I did for her.

I was a fucking coward when it comes to admitting that I cared about her while this guy didn't have that problem.

I pull Layla into my chest, and she arches her spine, circling her arm around my neck. I close my eyes, still not over the fact that Layla could actually be happy with a guy like that. A normal guy who didn't lose his eyesight, didn't have attachment issues, and didn't have the fear of failing to protect her.

But I have to keep my restlessness away because what's important now is her feelings. I know for sure that if Marco's punishment is executed, she will be heartbroken.

"You don't have to explain to him anymore about anything," I say.

She moves her head, and I can imagine her looking up at me with wonder.

"I'll talk to him, and you don't have to worry about anything," I say. "He'll be safe."

I make my way down into Black Wings jail with the thought of Layla still lingering in my head. The jail is located in the basement but lower level compared to where the boxing ring is placed.

The guys guarding the doors to the prisoner cells are already expecting me. One of them leads the way for me.

I'm glad that Layla is not here with me to go to the cell. It's not only because of my fear that Marco isn't in a proper emotional state to talk to her but also because this jail is not a good place for her. There are not many prisoners down here -- most of our traitors were usually killed as soon as possible -- but even though it's only a few of them here, their states are not for Layla's eyes.

While I'm walking through the hallway between the cells, I can hear one of the prisoners scream in agony through the torture and the other one beg for forgiveness over and over again. The prisoners left in our jail are the ones who get punished with slow and tortured death. The way they die depends on their sins and the extent of betrayal they committed.

Those two prisoners were taken because of Fenrir's order. Jaxon, Cole, Levi, and I didn't put people in our jail. The three of them were busy with way more important missions while I basically didn't care about our members, not until Layla came and turned my world upside down.

Now, here I am, walking inside our jail to talk to the prisoner I just put in yesterday. However, I specifically gave an order to not touch him until I speak to him, so Marco should be doing fine.

The answer should greet me when I finally stop in front of Marco's cell.

"He's doing fine," the guard tells me, knowing that I can't fucking see whether it's dark or not. "His ankle is chained, but even in this darkness, I can see that he's doing okay."

I nod, but then the alarm in my head suddenly rings as the guard makes an abrupt movement toward the cell.

"Wait." His voice is filled with fear. "He can't be... oh my God."

My heart is beating so fast when he quickly unlocks the cell and rushes toward Marco.

"Fuck," he curses. "Fuck."

"What the fuck is happening?" I ask impatiently.

"I thought that he was fine, until I saw the saliva dripping from his mouth."

I step closer to the cell, and a horrible feeling stirs inside me.

The guard moves, sounding like he's trying to find Marco's pulse. "Shit. He's gone."

For a second, I think that the world stops moving.

"How the fuck did that happen?" I boom, so loudly, I'm sure that the entire prison can hear me.

"I don't know." He pants, sounding as panicked as I am. "Maybe he assumed that he was going to be punished for his betrayal. I swear, he was still alive the last time I checked him. Oh, shit," he curses again, sounding like he just remembered something important. "He must have taken the poison from his friends when they visited him."

My heart sinks so low.

Marco must have thought that drinking poison would be a better way to die than being tortured slowly and painfully. He didn't know that I wasn't going to do that to him.

My anger consumes me to the core. I feel like I'm going to explode.

"I'm sorry," the guard stutters. "I didn't know that he was going to kill himself. I should have told him that you meant no harm, but I wasn't even sure what you were going to do to him when you saw him again. He stabbed you. You are our king--"

"Enough." I grit my teeth.

"I should probably get the doctor," he stutters again. "I mean, I checked him, but I can't be sure. I'll go get the doctor now."

I hear him running back toward the exit while I'm trying to figure out what to do. As much as I don't want Marco to die, the truth is the truth. I just can't imagine what Layla would feel if she knew about this.

"Fuck." I punch the ground of the cell with my fist, not caring that my knuckles bleed.

I stand up and make my way out of the prison. I stumble a few times because I've never been familiar enough with the corridor. When I almost reach the end of it, I hear a ruckus.

"What do you mean that he's dead?" someone snaps, his voice holding so much fear. "My brother is still alive."

I remember hearing this voice before, inside the boxing ring, after Marco stabbed me with the knife. Apparently, it's his brother. He sounds even more panicked now than the last time I heard his voice.

"It's a suicide," the guard says with guilt present in his voice. "He poisoned himself."

"What?" the brother's voice breaks, and I can almost feel his pain.

"He what?" another voice echoes, and my breath catches in my throat.

I know who this voice belongs to.

"Layla," I whisper in disbelief.

I told her not to come with me, but she must have followed me because of her worry.

Before I can proceed to make my presence known to all of them, Marco's brother hisses, "You filthy bitch. It's because of you that he died."

I stride with anger boiling my blood.

"No." Layla sounds like she's bursting into tears.

"You fucking manipulator." Marco's brother sounds like he wants to kill her. "You'll fucking pay for this one, you--"

I grab him before he can finish his sentence. I wrap my fingers around his throat, putting pressure with my tight grip. "Watch your mouth," I hiss. "Do not speak to her like that. You better fucking apologize to her."

It takes everything in me to not choke him. The only thing saving him from my wrath is the fact that his brother just died. I can understand his anger because I have a brother too. I don't know what I will do if the same thing happens to Jackson.

I loosen my grip on him and let him go. He pants heavily, but he doesn't say anything back.

The sound of Layla's footsteps rushing outside makes me snap around. Worry consumes me when I follow the sound of her shoes stomping on the ground.

"Layla," I shout. "Wait."

But she doesn't listen to me. She keeps running, and I keep chasing her like my life depends on it. The direction she goes in lets me know that we're heading toward the ground floor.

I'm sure that we reach the backyard when I feel the afternoon breeze blowing through my skin and the rays of sun touching my face. I follow Layla until I hear the sound of water from the fountain.

Her footsteps stop, and I know from the sound of her knees dropping to the ground that she's crying in front of the fountain with her head lying on the edge of it.

I freeze on the spot. Hearing her cries again petrifies me. Her sobs break, and my heart shatters even more. My hands are shaking on my sides because I feel like falling apart too.

"It's my fault," she whispers heartbrokenly. "He died, and it's because of me."

"No," I say firmly, more like angrily. My voice is also shaking because of the pain I feel for her. I engulf her in a tight embrace from behind. "Please don't say that," I rasp.

I feel her tears on my skin when our cheeks touch. I can taste her tears, and it's not only on my lips but also in my heart. It tastes like a bitter punishment.

"It was never your fault," I say, swallowing a lump in my throat.

If it's anyone's fault, it's mine.

If I hadn't been an ass in the beginning, she wouldn't have sought comfort in anyone else.

If I had been a great man and leader who could protect my fighters, he wouldn't have doubted me and thought of me as a horrible human being.

If I hadn't been blind, he might have believed that I could protect her.

Layla keeps crying in my arms while I keep hugging her from behind. The mixture of the sound of her crying and the water from the fountain creates harmony in the silent afternoon.

I'm silent, but in my head, Marco's voice echoes very clearly, as though the dead man is watching us and trying to warn me.

You can't protect her.

She's too good for you.

You can't make her happy.

Layla places her hands over mine circling her waist and grips them like I'm her everything.

"It's okay to let it go," I say. "Cry. Cry, Layla, as much as you want. I'll be here."

Her sobs break even more as I say that. I hold her even tighter.

I'm sorry.

I'm so fucking sorry.

I keep echoing those words in my heart over and over again. I can't say them out loud. It's useless. My apology can't be compared to the tears running down her face.

Nothing is worth her tears.

Nothing.

21

CHAPTER 21

LAYLA

Another day has passed.

A tear falls from my eye as I wash my face. I sniffle, still thinking about how Marco died. When I pat my face with a towel, I stare at the mirror and find my eyes puffy because of crying.

Even though Kellan held me all night long, it still didn't erase the pain in my heart.

It's devastating enough to find out that someone I know committed suicide, and it feels even more horrible that I had a part in that.

I didn't mean to make Marco feel like he lost the only person who understood what it was like to be put in a place where we felt we didn't belong, where everyone else but us would kill to be a part of it.

I brush my teeth, trying to distract my mind with something else, but it's no use.

After finishing my morning routine, I step out of the bathroom. My legs stop short as I find Kellan already waiting for me. He stands there in front of the bathroom, facing me.

The serious look on his hardened face makes me taken aback. He looks like he has something important to tell me. Dead important.

My heart beats faster. I don't think that I can take another bad news.

"Boxing ring," he says.

I'm at a loss for words.

"Let's go there." The way he says it leaves no room to argue, like he will carry me there if I refuse to go with him.

"The ring?" I can't help but ask.

Kellan turns around, expecting me to follow suit, and I do.

"Why?" I ask again, trying to catch up with his long strides.

I can only see his back, but I can imagine the deadly look crossing his expression while we're walking down the hallway. It's still very early in the morning, so it's quite deserted. Most people here party until late at night in the main part of the house and wake up only a few hours from now because of too much drinking.

"Do you think that I will just let it go after hearing what his brother said to you last night?" he speaks through gritted teeth.

My heart sinks as I remember how Marco's brother threatened me -- he told me that I should pay for his brother's death. Chills run through my skin as I think about what he will do to me.

Yet, talking to him and explaining to him that I cared about his brother seem like a bad idea. He must hate me to the point that he wants me dead.

In no time, we reach the basement where Kellan usually practices martial arts. My eyes land on the boxing ring, wondering what Kellan will do.

Why is he taking me here?

Kellan takes off his shirt and tosses it down before he even stops walking. Then he turns around to face me, clenching his jaw.

I'm still panting because of rushing here.

"Follow me," he says in a commanding tone, stepping onto the ring.

He stretches out his arm to help me get on to it too, and I let him drag me up.

I'm starting to understand where this is going, but I don't think that I'm ready. Kellan, however, seems like he's in a hurry, as if there's nothing else more important now than to bring me here. Still, I think that he's rushing it. I'm not prepared for it.

"I'm going to train you," he says.

I swallow.

"You heard him. I can't get it out of my head. He's going to hurt you, Layla."

"Kellan--"

"I can't always protect you," he interrupts before I can even speak my mind. "He knows he will be dead if he ever touches you, but he's still going to do it."

The anger radiating from his body is unmistakable. I can see how the situation is shaking him. His fists are clenched tightly on his sides. His chest heaves up and down.

"I'm going to hunt him if he ever dares go near you, but I'm not fucking risk it," he says firmly. "You have to learn how to defend yourself. I can't fucking see, Layla."

I step forward. "Kellan--"

"You're going to start now," he urges. "You're going to fight me as if I were him, and I'm going to teach you to protect yourself."

Without waiting for my response, Kellan strides towards the center of the ring. The menacing look on his face tells me to approach him, and I reluctantly do it.

I look down at myself. I'm wearing my jogger and T-shirt today. Maybe it should be enough to accommodate my movement, but I am nowhere near pro. I can't even say that I'm an athletic person. I only exercise regularly for my health. If one should ask how well I exercise or participate in sports, I have no doubt that I am below average. That's something that I still have to fix.

I gulp and take a deep breath. I want to tell him to not panic and that Marco's brother might just have given me an empty threat, but it seems too late now.

Kellan guides me through the warm-ups, and when it's time to practice, I can't help but become more nervous.

"We'll start now," Kellan says. "I'm going to teach you how to punch, block and kick."

I watch as Kellan gives me the examples. He does it with so much precision that I wonder if I will ever do it right. He's just too good. The impact of his movement on his enemies is fatal, but he makes it look so easy for him.

When it's time for me to do it, he follows closely and guides me through the movement.

"You're doing it wrong," he hisses, as though my mistakes frustrate him to the core. "Make sure that your elbow is not locked. Pull the fist that is not punching back. If you don't do it right, your punch won't be strong. Again."

I pant, trying my best to do it right. It feels impossible to do it perfectly. I wish he could spare me because it's the first time for me to learn how to fight. But Kellan is persistent. He won't stop until I get it right.

I don't even know how long time has passed since we entered the basement.

"Again," he commands.

We have moved to another step because I couldn't nail my punc h.He's now teaching me how to block my enemy's attack, and again, I keep failing miserably.

How could I win if he was the one who attacked me? He's a freaking champion.

He brings me down again but then impatiently tells me to get up for the thousandth time. I don't even know it anymore. I've lost count.

"Again, Layla," he snaps and turns his back to me, preparing for another round.

My heart hurts because of the way he speaks to me.

"I can't," I finally shout, throwing my hands in the air as I stand up. "I can't do this. You're being too aggressive. How can I defeat someone like you?"

My chest rises and falls, but then my voice softens, "Just, please. Turn it down a little." I sound helpless, literally begging him.

"No," he growls. His body is shaking with anger. "Are you crazy? Someone who attacks you may want to kill you. He's not going to back down," he hollers, his eyes wide in fury.

I never saw Kellan this angry, and I've seen him angry a lot. We have to stop this. This is not good. This is hurting him too, maybe even more than it is hurting me.

"I haven't even mastered my stance," I say. "This is crazy, Kellan. I can't do it like this. Why don't we take it slow?"

"Because we have no fucking time," he booms, so loudly that his voice is echoing in the basement.

I stare at him in shock, watching him explode. His eyes are red, and the way he's breathing makes me afraid. It's like he can have a heart attack anytime now.

He's not panting because of the physical exercise. It's because of his anger and fear.

"Again, Layla," he says curtly.

Tears pool in my eyes. I feel so tired and bruised and broken, that I may collapse anytime. My head pulses with sharp pain, and the room is spinning.

Is it already dark outside?

For God knows how many times, I fall onto the ground again, unable to defend myself against Kellan's attack. This time, I can't get up again. I can't even move my cheek off the cold cement.

I'm drained, physically and mentally.

"Get up." Kellan's voice is shaking.

I can hear his fear very clearly. I can even feel it all over my bruised body.

"Get up, Layla," he roars.

I close my eyes, letting my tears fall. I can taste it in my mouth while I'm lying here on the ground. My body might be hurting, but it hurts more to see him like this.

Kellan...

You're the one who said that you were not my hero.

Why are you trying so hard to protect me, to the point that it hurts both of us like this?

"Layla." His voice cracks. "Get up. Try it one more time. Just one more time." His voice turns into a pained whisper. "Try not to die."

But I'm already dying.

"It hurts," I cry softly. "I can't even move my body. Kellan--" I finally let my sob break.

Kellan rushes toward me and gets down on his knees. He turns my body so that I can lie down with my back on his lap. He wraps his arms around me.

"Fuck. I'm sorry." His eyes are glassy, and I swallow a lump in my throat. "I'm sorry, Layla," he rasps.

"I--"

"Sshh," he cuts me off. "No need to speak."

His eyes are filled with guilt and sorrow. The sight breaks me. I want to see the light in them again.

"Just rest," he says. "I'm going to take care of you."

I sigh, feeling him tighten his hold on me.

Before I know it, I'm drifting off.

22

CHAPTER 22

KELLAN

I sit on my bed, caressing Layla's hair. She hasn't woken up yet. She only stirs against my touch.

It's still too early in the morning, so I'm not planning to wake her up soon. She still needs to rest.

Yesterday, I drilled her in the boxing ring, and it was too much. I knew that I was being too hard on her, but I was fucking scared. All I could think about was losing her.

When I first met her, I already knew that this place might only bring her danger, and after what happened recently, my fear heightened even more.

If I can't protect her...

My eyes squeeze shut the moment the thought crosses my mind. It's my biggest fear now, and it's eating me because I know that it's very possible to happen.

I stand up, preparing to go for my morning jog. I want to spend every second with her because it's the only way for me to ensure that she's safe, but with what I did to her yesterday, I need to think clearly.

I don't want today to end like yesterday. I don't want to push her too hard to the point that I hurt her again. I need this morning jog to clear my mind first and let out all this restlessness inside my body.

I kiss Layla's hair and sigh. As I pull away, I remember how I tried to ease her pain yesterday and how much she liked it.

Last night, I let her rest on the bed and gave her a little massage on the legs and arms. I knew that she was hurting, so I did my best to make it better.

The smell of the aromatherapy oil is still filling the room, and I'm glad that it can continue to help her relax for a little more. I will only wake her up when it's time for breakfast.

LAYLA

My eyelids flicker as I feel the rays of the sun tickling the skin of my face. I slowly open my eyes, stretching my arms.

God, my body feels sore because of too much practice yesterday.

I roll onto my side, expecting to see Kellan still lying beside me. But to my disappointment, he's already gone.

I sit up on the bed, hugging my knees as I think about what we're going to do today. A smile curves on the corner of my mouth as my gaze darts to the aromatherapy candles sitting on the nightstand. I appreciate the little things he did for me to make me feel better. It's funny to witness someone who can be so grumpy and intimidating suddenly flipping to doing sweet things like that.

I lean back against the headboard and grab my phone from the other nightstand. One voice message greets me, and I smile again as I see the sender's name. It's Kellan.

I press the message to hear his voice, wondering about what he wanted to say earlier when I was still asleep.

"Hey, I'm taking a jog for a while. I didn't want to wake you up. I locked the door when I left the room because I wanted you to be safe. Wait for me until I come back. In case of emergency, I put the spare keys on the desk."

I see that he's being extra careful, but I understand why he's doing all of this.

Lazily, I get up from the bed and walk into the bathroom to brush my teeth and wash my face. As usual, I hum and sing while doing this morning routine. I wonder if Kellan has ever felt annoyed by this.

As soon as I realize that, I stop my movement, staring into the mirror. But then, I shrug and continue brushing my teeth. He already said that I was annoying, anyway.

When I walk out of the bathroom, I hear a knock on the door. A grin immediately creeps on my lips. I'm glad that Kellan has finished his morning jog because I'm already hungry. I can't wait to have breakfast with him.

"Coming." I grab the keys while passing the desk and totter toward the door.

When I open it, I see no one.

My brows furrow in confusion. But then, I realize what I just did, and my heart skips a beat.

Why would Kellan knock on the door? He had the keys. He said that he locked me up from outside because he wanted me to be safe.

The spare keys are for emergencies.

Abruptly, I snap my body around, rushing back into the room. But before I can close the door, someone's arm suddenly circles my waist. Their hand covers my mouth to muffle my scream.

The person shuts the door behind me, and panic consumes me. I struggle to break free, trying to scream. My attacker squeezes my mouth to keep me quiet.

"Shut the fuck up," a cold voice hisses in my ear, and I remember who it belongs to.

Marco's brother.

I kick his foot, elbow his stomach, and grip his hands in an attempt to break free, but he's so much more powerful than me. His grip on me is limiting my movement.

My mind turns blank as I try to remember what Kellan taught me to defend myself. But fear is the only thing I can feel now, it clouds my mind.

Marco's brother flips me over and throws me onto the bed. I lie on my back while he towers over me. To my horror, his hands shoot to my throat, wrapping it tightly and choking me.

My eyes widen. All I can see is the rage skating all over his face.

"I don't care what you are to Kellan." His nostrils flare, and his eyes are red, filled with fury. "Did you think that you could just go on with your life after what happened to my brother?"

Tears well up in my eyes. It's not only because of the pain in my heart but also because of gradually losing my breath. I grip his hands with all my power to release his grip from my throat, my nails dug into his skin.

"If he hadn't been put into jail because of you, he wouldn't have taken the poison from Luca," he lashes out.

I stare at him in disbelief.

Luca?

Luca was the one who gave Marco the poison?

Anger builds up inside me, and my instinct to survive makes me muster all the energy left in me to land a hard kick into his chest. The sudden attack causes him to release me, but it's only for a moment.

While I'm still trying to breathe properly, he grabs my collar. He throws me sideways, causing me to crash the nightstand. It topples, falling onto the ground. I land on the floor harshly while the aromatherapy candles crash into the bookshelf.

The candles, mixed with the oil, make contact with the papers and start to create fire before my eyes.

I feel like the world suddenly stops moving, but before I can do something about it, Marco's brother is suddenly on me again, straddling me. He traps my wrists with his hands, locking them on my sides.

He clenches his jaw. "I don't fucking understand what you did to him. He attacked Kellan because of you. He committed suicide. Why? He was doing fine before you came around."

Pain sips into my heart again as I realize that he doesn't even know his brother's struggle.

"I gave him money." Grudge is laced in his words. "I gave him a fucking good job. He was chosen for a mission that would make him fucking proud. Why. Why?"

"Because he was suffering," I scream, unable to hold it back any longer.

It's going to hurt him, but he has to know what Marco really felt.

"He hated his life here," I say. "He didn't want to be here. He felt like he didn't belong."

It looks like my words are a punch into his heart because he suddenly freezes. The anger is still very much visible in his eyes.

I swallow. "He never wanted to be a part of Black Wings. He hated the people here. He hated the mission," I cry, remembering the words Marco said to me the last time I saw him. "He didn't want to kill--"

"Shut up," he barks. "You know nothing about my brother. Do not speak as if he had any problem before you happened."

Tears are rolling down my cheeks.

But it was the truth.

I only made it worse because I made him feel even more lonely than before. I was the only one whom he thought would understand him. He thought that it would be the two of us against the darkness around us.

Marco's words echo again inside my head, and I squeeze my eyes shut.

"We're the same, Layla. I see myself when I see you. We're not supposed to turn into them. We're better than them."

When I open my eyes, all I can see is his brother's rage again. Before I know it, he slaps me hard across my face. The blow is so painful that I can't help but curl myself on the floor.

I watch as he arches his spine. He sits on his knees and closes his eyes. He takes a deep breath, as though he's trying to forget my words.

My vision becomes more blurry, not only because of my tears but also because of the smoke starting to fill the room. The fire has begun to spread, and my heart kicks up a notch.

With difficulty, I stand on my feet and drag my legs to the balcony. Just when I touch the railing, I am pushed against it. He grabs a handful of my hair with his fist and forces me to turn around to face him. With his other hand, he grips my throat again.

I choke, unable to bear the pain. I haven't even recovered from his first attempt to choke me to death.

My feet are lifted from the ground, and my back arches to the point that I can fall over the balcony if he pushes me just a little bit.

I don't know which one will be a more painful way to die -- choked to death or falling over the balcony.

I wish that somebody, anybody, would catch sight of us from down below and help me.

My thoughts are running wild inside my head. The reality that I may really die today forces my adrenaline to rush.

No. I can't die. Not now.

What about Kellan?

What about my family?

I struggle for my life, kicking and punching in every direction. I manage to knee him at the right spot, making him groan and lose his grip on me. I take that split second to free myself from his hold and rush back into the room although it's practically burning.

I can hear him curse behind me. Just when I glance back, the other bookshelf that has caught fire topples to the ground, falling over him. His painful scream rings in my ears as I stumble forward. I fall onto the floor and crawl with my elbows.

I glance back again. My eyes widen as I watch the fire consume him.

"No," I whisper in fear.

Although he can't hurt me anymore, it's still a horrible thing to watch someone dying before my very eyes.

The heat is killing me. The smoke is becoming worse. My eyes hurt.

The more seconds pass, the more it's getting harder to breathe inside the room. I don't know what I should do and where I should go. The fire has caught the door as well, and when I stare up at the ceiling, it seems like a part of it can collapse at any time.

I never felt so close to death.

23

CHAPTER 23

K ELLAN

After I finish my morning jog, I walk back to the house, thinking about my schedule today with Layla. I have to train her again. I know that we have to do it every day until she can master her defense. It may not fully prevent her from danger, but it's the least I can give her.

While I'm getting closer to the house, I stop in my tracks. There's something wrong with the air I breathe. It's bitter, and it smells like smoke.

The wind blows harsher, making it even more obvious. My mind is immediately on alert.

There's a fire, and judging from the direction of the wind, it's coming from the house.

My heart beats like a drum in my chest as I speed up my pace. I'm now running, my breath short and fast due to the sudden panic building up inside me.

"There's a fire on the third floor," someone shouts.

Before I can reach inside the house, I'm already blocked by people surrounding the side of the mansion. Their gasps and murmurs let me know that they are trying to figure out what's happening.

"Shit. Isn't that Kellan's room?" a guy asks, and my heart almost stops.

"I saw it," a girl yells. "I saw them on the balcony. He was trying to choke her."

"Are you sure about that?" someone else asks in disbelief.

"What the fuck is happening?" I snap.

The noises around me turn quiet in an instant. The air is thick with fear.

"Kellan," another guy stutters, as though he can't believe that I have reached here.

"Answer me," I boom, my whole body shaking.

The way I'm panting hard is not even healthy. I can't breathe. It's like the air in my lungs is being sucked forcefully.

I don't know what I will do if something bad indeed happened to Layla. And judging from what I just heard, it wasn't just bad. It's enough to make me want to destroy the entire world.

"Kellan," someone starts, sounding extremely nervous. "It's your room--" He can't even finish his sentence.

I'm still panting like I'm about to collapse. I'm sure that they all can hear my ragged breathing. I don't even ask him to keep talking because I can't even utter a single word now with how rapidly I'm breathing.

"It's on fire," someone else finishes the sentence.

"Layla." My voice is shaking uncontrollably, I almost choke. "Where is she?"

No one can answer me. I can only hear silence, and it's like a knife slicing my heart very slowly.

"Where the hell is she?" I roar.

My hands, down to the tip of my fingers, are trembling in fear.

Just now, I did hear that someone broke into my room and planned to choke her to death.

I can guess who it is, and I will kill him with my bare hands.

I grit my teeth, storming in the direction of the house, but then someone catches me, blocking me from the entrance.

"Kellan." It's Stas. He pushes my body back with his bulky one, gripping my upper arms. "You can't go in there."

I push him back, feeling like I can explode. "Get off me."

"Goddammit," Stas speaks through clenched teeth, struggling to hold me back. "Everyone, come over here right now," he shouts to the people around us. "Help me hold him back. Protect him."

"Get the fuck off," I lash out as more people hold me back. They grab my arms and lock my waist.

Protect me?

Here I am, being protected as their king, but I can't do anything to protect her.

"Get off me, you fucking people," I holler with rage evident in my tone. "I'm going to kill you all if you don't let me go inside."

"And Jaxon will punish us all if we let you," Stas snaps, making me freeze. "Your brother wouldn't want you to go inside, Kellan. What are you going to do there? I'm so fucking sorry that I have to say this to you, but--"

He takes a deep breath, bracing to say the next words that are going to hurt me.

"You have no sight. You can't just expect yourself to save her from the fire. Are you just going to blindly force your way through the fire and let us risk both of you dying?"

I feel the tears in my eyes even before Stas finishes his sentence.

Goddammit, I know it.

I fucking know that I'm fucking blind.

But I have to save her.

The ugly truth has just been thrown at me. Even when I don't mind dying, even when I indeed die in the process, what if I still can't save her?

My body goes rigid because of the pain consuming me.

Stas sighs, and I can hear Zoe's cries somewhere in the background.

Stas grabs my shoulder to assure me. "You are our king, Kellan. It is our job to help you fulfill what you need. Stay here. I'm going to look for her, and I promise you, I will do my best to save her."

Before I can respond, I hear his footsteps running toward the house. And just like that, he's gone to save Layla.

My teeth are chattering due to the mixture of fear, anger, and sadness stirring inside me. The people are still holding me back, but I'm no longer struggling to get away. I can only stare ahead with hope that Layla will come back to me.

I unknowingly let my tear fall, followed by another, and another.

People shout around me, trying to find a way to put the fire down. Some people have already called for help to extinguish the fire. The others are talking loudly with urgency in their tones.

It's chaos around me, but it's nothing compared to the turmoil in my heart.

I'm standing here, unable to do anything. I can only freeze on the spot.

Waiting.

Waiting.

And still, waiting.

The sound of the fire burning fills the air, and I don't think that I'll ever forget it for the rest of my life.

This is another nightmare.

I'm being left in the dark again.

With no sight.

No choices.

No chances.

No hope for me to protect the person dear to me.

I can only accept whatever the pain that will engulf me.

On the day that Layla Hayes might be dying, I can only blindly search for a miracle.

24

CHAPTER 24

LAYLA

My eyelids feel so heavy when I try to open my eyes. Slowly, I try again, and when I finally open them, I'm greeted by a white ceiling.

I squint, my eyes still adjusting to the overwhelming light. Gradually, my vision becomes better.

I look around and find myself lying on the bed inside a room surrounded by white walls. Other than this bed, there is only a small cupboard, a desk with a chair, and an IV pole next to me.

This is a room to treat a patient, but it doesn't look like a hospital room. It looks more like a clinic.

I abruptly sit up as what happened in Kellan's room flashes back in my mind. My heart suddenly beats faster, causing me to grip my chest over the thin fabric of the robe.

The last thing I remember is losing consciousness inside the bathroom when the fire spread even worse. Did I just survive it?

What about Marco's brother? Is he dead?

Movement from the door startles me. I find Zoe standing in the doorway with her eyes wide in surprise. She hurriedly totters toward me and engulfs me in a tight hug. When she pulls away, I see the tears of relief in her eyes. She gives me a warm smile and holds my hands.

"You're awake." A man's voice makes me turn my head toward the door again.

Stas approaches me, and I can see the same relief in his expression.

"How..." I don't even know how to ask. There are so many questions in my head, and my heart is not ready yet to tell them how I almost got killed.

"You got us all worried," Stas sighs. "But it's all over now. After I got into the room, I found you lying unconscious on the bathroom floor. Luckily, the fire hadn't spread there as much as the other parts of the room. I managed to get you out just in time before the ceiling dropped."

I shiver after listening to him. It feels surreal that I just got out of that kind of nightmare.

Stas squeezes Zoe's shoulder to comfort her and stares at her tenderly while Zoe sighs. She must have been worried to death about her father.

"Thank you for saving me," I whisper.

My eyes water because of how grateful I am. I owe Stas my life.

"Anytime, Layla." Stas smiles.

I'm so glad that I have the two of them here in Black Wings. They are so kind and warm, unlike the other members.

Kellan once told me that they were considered a part of the family, since Stas had been working in the mansion for a long time. He and Zoe came before Kellan's parents died.

"Layla," another voice echoes from the door, and my heart skips a beat. Kellan is standing by the door.

He must have heard my voice.

"You're awake?" His expression is a mixture of disbelief and hope.

But what makes my breath catch in my throat are his eyes. They hold so much sadness. Looking at him like this makes me want to cry.

Stas and Zoe exchange looks and nod. "Well then, we're just going to head out," he says.

I straighten up. Before I can ask the question lingering in my head, Stas says, "This is Doctor Dezzani's clinic. You're still in Black Wings mansion. He will check you up in a few minutes. As far as I heard, there's nothing to worry about your condition, but he'll explain to you better."

I nod, watching as he and Zoe excuse themselves and head to the door.

Kellan walks toward me and takes a seat beside the bed. I instantly reach for his hand, and he holds mine.

"How are you feeling?" he asks, concern written all over his face.

"I feel okay." I clear my throat, not wanting him to worry.

I touch my neck with the back of my other hand. It still hurts, and I bet that there are marks because of how hard I was choked. But I'm sure that it will heal.

Kellan doesn't ask me about my attacker, so I figure that he already knew who it was.

"Is he--"

Kellan quickly releases his hold on my hand the second he hears what I'm about to ask. He balls his fist instead until his knuckles turn white and clenches his jaw.

"Dead," he says coldly. "Burnt to death."

I gasp, shooting my hand to my mouth. "Oh, God."

"It's still nothing compared to what he has done to you," Kellan speaks in a low voice, and his tone makes me shudder. "He was lucky that he was dead because if he hadn't been, I would have made his death a slow and painful one. I would have tortured him--"

"Kellan," I interrupt, holding his hand again.

His eyes soften, and the tension on his shoulders eases.

"It's over," I say. "I don't want to think about it anymore."

He sighs, squeezing my hand. I place my other hand on his cheek, making him turn his face toward me. He sighs again and places a soft kiss on my palm, creating butterflies inside my tummy.

"I'm okay now," I say. "Are you?"

He swallows. His reaction makes me frown. I watch as the muscles on his neck move. I need to hear that he's okay too, but he doesn't give me that answer.

I know that he's still not over the fact that I was attacked while he was away, but I survived.

Please, Kellan. Say something. Tell me what you feel, what you're worried about. Tell me the truth, and don't shut off.

My thumb caresses his cheek, and he holds my hand, stopping me.

"Do you want to go somewhere?" he asks out of the blue.

I don't know what to answer. It sounds like he still has more to say.

"You said that you didn't want to think about it anymore. Should we take a vacation?" His brows furrow.

My mouth hangs open.

I wouldn't have dreamt that Kellan Romero would ask me to go on a vacation with him.

"What?" I whisper. "But I thought that we're not allowed to go out unless we're on a mission."

Kellan shakes his head, and I'm surprised to find amusement in his eyes. "It doesn't apply to the leaders. You couldn't possibly think so."

I suddenly feel stupid. I'm still at a loss for words. The idea of getting out of this suffocating place -- even just for a while -- is too good.

I can't help but ask, "Where do you want us to go?"

"A place where my family used to go," Kellan says.

I can hear from the way he said it that he treasures it. It must be a memorable place for him and his family.

"I haven't gone there again for quite a while," he says. "I think it's about time for me to go there again."

A soft smile touches my lips. If going to such a place can make Kellan happy, I will go there in a heartbeat.

It's good timing for me too, considering what just happened to me. This trip with Kellan sounds like a perfect treat.

"So, what do you think, Layla?" Kellan asks, squeezing my hand on his cheek. "Do you want to go with me?"

I chuckle, feeling warmth in my heart. Another smile forms on my lips. "Of course. I'd love to."

25

Chapter 25

L AYLA

I stare out the window as the car brings us to our destination. Stas is driving while Zoe is in the front passenger seat. Kellan and I sit at the back.

It's refreshing to see the town again after being caged in the mansion. My eyes follow the people walking on the pavement and the building we pass. It's nice to witness the normal lifestyle again after a long time.

Our journey takes hours, and as time goes by, our surroundings change into somewhere deserted again. Now that we've left the town, my anticipation builds up. I have a feeling that we're going to reach our destination soon.

As the car slows down, my gaze darts to a beautiful lake surrounded by forest and hills. I gasp and snap my head toward Kellan.

"Kellan." My voice is filled with excitement, which he only responds with a nod.

A smile creeps on my lips as my eyes land on a cabin standing next to the lake. To say that this place is beautiful is an understatement. The lake is clear as glass. The wooden cabin is located next to the outdoor space that features a lawn filled with large vegetation and a fire pit. The beautiful lake is the backyard.

After Stas parks the car, the four of us get out of it. Stas and Zoe help us pull out our luggage and bring them into the cabin.

"Well then, just call us if you need anything," Stas says to us, already preparing to leave.

I frown. "Why so soon? Aren't you guys going to join us for a while? We can have a grill near the lake," I say, thinking that it might be the perfect plan for all of us. I'm sure that Stas and Zoe feel tired because of the journey.

Zoe smiles, shaking her head in disagreement.

"Nah, that's okay." Stas pats my shoulder. "We've got work to do. Fenrir just recruited some new members today, and they need us."

My shoulders sag. I can't help but wonder about Fenrir. I haven't met him, but it's clear that most of the members living in the mansion were recruited by him.

"I'll be here again next week to pick you up." He pats Kellan's shoulder.

Kellan just nods, and I watch as they get into the car.

After they leave, Kellan and I step into the cabin. I can't help but travel my eyes around the place with awe.

The living area is equipped with comfortable furniture and a fireplace. I can see why it creates the perfect spot for relaxation for Kellan's family. Even though it's not that spacious, it has enough space to sit the entire family, and if they'd like to dine with a view, they can always head to the deck where there's an outdoor area overlooking the lake.

There's also a well-equipped kitchen -- I can imagine Kellan's mother using it to treat everyone to memorable meals and snacks.

"This place is beautiful," I whisper.

I turn to Kellan, wondering how he feels about this. He can no longer see his surroundings, but I wonder if he can remember the feeling of being here.

He closes his eyes, taking a deep breath. "It still feels the same. The smell of the air, the woods, and the lake," he stops mid-sentence, as if he's reminiscing everything, "the feel of the wooden floor against my feet. I still remember that Jaxon, Inez, and I used to run around here. I remember Jaxon and I tormenting each other, Inez laughing, and our mother scolding us. My father is not an affectionate person, but he would listen to us all."

There's sadness in his eyes when he opens them. I can't help but hold his hand.

"It's all a memory, but it feels good," Kellan says, causing relief to wash over me. "It feels good to be back here."

"This place doesn't feel abandoned," I mumble.

The cabin is pretty clean despite the fact that it hasn't been used for years.

Kellan sighs. "Jaxon always makes sure that this place is cleaned regularly. He paid someone to do that."

Kellan steps in the direction of the patio. I follow him, guiding him toward it because he still needs to readjust to his surroundings after all these years.

The wind blows through our skin the moment our feet step on the outdoor area at the back of the cabin. The deck overlooking the lake has a passage for us to walk closer to the water, and I almost cry because of how beautiful the sight is.

I stare at Kellan, wishing that he could see this again.

"Will you help me walk toward the end of the deck?" he asks.

"Of course," I say and do as he says.

While we're walking along the wooden concrete, he asks, "It's about time for sunset, isn't it?"

I stare at the sky, and indeed, it's about time that the sun sets.

I hold Kellan's hand tightly while we're walking closer to the end of the deck. The water is already on our sides, so I have to be careful to not let him fall.

We stop and sit at the end of it to enjoy the moment. I dip my toe into the water. It's not that cold, just the perfect temperature.

I lay my head on Kellan's shoulder, staring at the view before us and wishing again that a miracle would happen so that he could get his sight back. I unknowingly let a tear fall from my eye because of this overwhelming feeling, and I'm afraid that he will notice it because it drops on his shoulder.

"Tell me about it," he says as I secretly wipe my eye and straighten up. "Tell me about the sunset. What do you see? Is it still as beautiful as I remember?"

I never heard Kellan say the word beautiful before -- the word seems too flowery for a person with a cold exterior like him -- so the sunset here must be really special for him. Of course, he used to watch it with the people he loved -- his family.

"It still is." I gaze at the sunset.

He can't see it, so I'm trying my best to describe it.

"The sky is changing colors, and the sun is getting closer to the horizon," I say. "The golden disc almost touches the surface of the water. The color of the sky is a mixture of orange, yellow, and flamboyant pink. It's vivid, but not too bright. Just gazing at it makes me feel warm."

I inhale the air around me, feeling my chest tighten. Kellan gazes at the sky, in the same direction, but I don't know what he's thinking about. He doesn't look sad. Instead, he looks as if he's contented. I expect him to smile in any second, but it doesn't happen.

"I've been seeing black for such a long time," he says. "I can no longer remember the colors."

My heart feels like it's falling into a pit. My eyes start to brim with tears again.

As if he can understand how devastated I am after hearing that, Kellan places his palm on my cheek and shakes his head.

"Don't be sad for me." He stares into me, his voice hoarse. "You get to see how beautiful it is, and that's why I brought you here. I want you to see it, Layla. I want you to see it for me."

I hold his hand on my cheek. "Do you miss it?" I whisper brokenly.

He nods. "I do. I do miss the sunset that I can no longer see. But I don't need it anymore, especially now."

The corner of his lips curves up, and I wonder if I'm imagining it.

Yet, Kellan indeed looks contented. He doesn't seem as sad as I am.

He turns his head toward the water. "I always wanted to come here again, but Jaxon was always busy. I didn't want to come here alone. But now, I'm here with you."

I stare at him, thinking about how lonely he'd felt during all those years he waited for Jaxon.

"Layla," he whispers.

"Hm?"

He faces me again. "Do you think that my brother will ever come back home?"

I can feel the weight of his question pulling me down. It's a tough question to answer, but I know that I only have one answer. I haven't lost hope. I haven't lost my faith that Jaxon is still alive.

"Yes. I'm sure that he'll come back home," I say.

Kellan focuses his attention on the sky again although he can't see it. We stay silent for a long moment, feeling the breeze blowing softly against our skin. I sigh, allowing myself to cherish every second we have here before we go back into the cabin.

"You know," Kellan starts, tentatively, causing me to wonder what he's about to say. "If there's only one color I can remember again, I would kill to see it again."

He turns his face toward me, and strangely, now I can see the sadness in his eyes.

"It's blue."

26

CHAPTER 26

L AYLA

"I'm fucking hungry," Kellan grumbles while he's waiting for his dinner to be served.

He's sitting at the dining table, and the aroma of the truffle I'm cooking for him has been making his hunger worse.

I chuckle, witnessing his grumpy attitude as I prepare his meal in the kitchen. "Just a little bit more. I told you to just wait in the bedroom or somewhere else. You don't have to sit there and torture yourself."

"I still can smell it from any room inside this house," he mutters.

I shake my head in amusement.

"God. I'm fucking getting out of here." He stands up from the chair and storms out to the patio.

I focus my attention back on the mushroom soup I've been cooking. It's going to be done really soon while the other dishes are already placed on the kitchen counter.

I glance at the honey-glazed chicken and potato gnocchi I made earlier. A proud smile touches my lips.

After I finish cooking, I turn off the stove. Since Kellan has already moved to the patio, it's better if we have the dinner there.

I bring the food to the other dining area located on the back patio, and Kellan immediately straightens up in his seat.

"I'm literally drooling," he growls. "What took you so long?"

I almost roll my eyes, but I can't help the small smile creeping on my lips. He might be a mafia leader, but sometimes he acts like a baby.

I feel slightly bad for making him wait so long, but the moment he devours my cooking like it's the best meal he's ever had in his life, I make a note to myself that the process is worth it.

"Fuck. You cooked all my favorite food."

I watch as he keeps eating with so much enthusiasm. It does something to my heart even though what we're doing now is a simple thing. Just to witness him being happy makes my heart leap in delight.

I realize now that seeing Kellan happy is another level of happiness for me. I don't know why it's so important to me. Maybe it's because he has suffered a lot and because I always think that he deserves more in life.

I've been so absorbed in watching him enjoy his meal that I barely touch my food. I clear my throat, feeling embarrassed of myself. My cheeks heat up, and I'm grateful that he can't see it.

While I'm eating quietly, he says, "You know, you didn't have to do that."

I look up from my plate and see him staring in my direction.

"You can cook any dishes you want, and I will devour it nonetheless," he says. "I love your cooking, whatever it is."

His words melt my heart.

Kellan has been really nice nowadays, and sometimes it still catches me off guard because of the way he used to be when we first met.

"I wanted to," I say truthfully, and his eyes soften.

Kellan leans back on his chair, since he has already finished eating. A longing crosses his expression, and the question is already on the tip of my tongue.

"Did you and your family spend a lot of time on this patio?" I ask.

It feels unbelievable that I used to be scared of asking about his family because of the scar that never faded in his heart, but now we can approach the topic rather casually. It makes me think that Kellan is indeed slowly healing. He's not consistently angry anymore. He still is, at times, but not unreasonably.

I hope he has realized that not all the vulnerable feelings he experiences are bad, just like when I ask him to dance in the rain. Losing his family is still a pain to him, but the memory of them is something that he should cherish rather than escape.

"Yes, we did spend a lot of time on this patio," Kellan finally says. "During the day, we would have an afternoon tea together. My parents would ask us what we had learned that day. Sometimes, Jaxon liked to show off the new martial arts move he recently mastered, and I would challenge him because I couldn't help being a cocky bastard. My parents would watch us with amusement, sitting together exactly on the spot we're sitting now, while Inez would be busy making a necklace of flowers on the ground."

I listen intently to his every word, not missing that his grey eyes light up while he's remembering the good times.

"My father was a busy man, but when we were here, he always made sure to focus on us," he says. "Then later at night, when it was time for us to sleep, he would ask my mother to dance in this patio. I caught them dancing a couple of times, but they were so lost in the moment that they didn't even notice me coming."

I smile, enjoying his story.

"When I was a kid, I always thought that I would never ask a girl to dance because it looked too intimate," he says. "It wasn't cool in my eyes. It's too girly."

I raise my eyebrows skeptically. "It wasn't cool?"

He shakes his head. "No, it wasn't."

"It's too girly?"

"It was." He cocks an eyebrow. "I would have felt emasculated."

"Emasculated?" I pretend to gasp.

"Yes." Amusement glints in his eyes. "Should I spell it out for you?"

To my surprise, I laugh out loud, enjoying the bickering.

"My goodness," I say. "You asked me to dance once in your room. Did you forget about that?"

He squints at me, looking genuinely confused. "I'm not sure about that. As far as I remember, you were the one who asked me to dance with you."

Oh, God. We're not doing this right now.

I'm about to counter his statement, but then I realize that I'm not so sure anymore about what was our conversation at that time.

"It doesn't matter now," I mutter but then lean forward over the table, resting my cheeks on my palms as I look at him playfully. "Ask me to dance."

Kellan licks his lips. Amusement becomes more visible in his expression. His eyes are smiling.

"Now?" he asks.

"Yeah."

"Without music?" he challenges.

I huff, tossing my phone onto the table. I search for the exact same song that was playing in his room when we did slow dancing before. Soon, the music fills the air, and I wait for him.

Kellan stands up from his chair and offers his hand to me. "May I?" he asks politely.

I can't hold my giggle. "My pleasure," I hum, letting him pull me up to my feet.

We settle into the basic position, and I tease, "So, you were sayi ng...?"

He scoffs. "Come on. I was a boy back then."

I raise my eyebrows. "And now?"

"I'm a man." He pulls me closer by the waist, and I collide with his chest.

With my hand in his and the other one on his shoulder, we start to dance.

"You've learned that I'm a terrible dancer," Kellan speaks close to my ear, sending shivers down my spine. "I'm not going to warn you."

I laugh again, throwing my head back. "Don't worry. I won't let you fall."

We dance slowly. Just like the last time, I guide him through the steps, and Kellan is already better than the last time we did this.

A contented smile curves on my lips. I rest my head on his chest, inhaling his masculine scent that brings me a sense of calmness.

We keep swaying. Just when I close my eyes, wondering if I can stay inside this bubble of happiness forever, I hear him whisper.

"But I already did."

27

CHAPTER 27

L AYLA

"It's supposed to be somewhere around here," Kellan says in an irritated tone.

Today, we're going to spend time in the hammock inside the woods. We've been walking for quite a while, but unfortunately, we still can't find it yet.

"As far as I remember, it's not that far," he mutters, and I can only sigh.

It's been ages since he went to that hammock -- and he hadn't lost his sight the last time he went there -- so I totally understand if he can't immediately find his way back there. Yet, as usual, Kellan is being too hard on himself.

"That's okay," I mumble. "I'm actually quite enjoying walking in this woods."

I travel my eyes around the forest, gazing at the beautiful redwoods and rust-colored trunks. The afternoon breeze blows softly, creating the rustling sound of the leaves.

Indeed, spending time with Kellan in the hammock would be a perfect way to spend our time until evening comes before we have dinner later at the cabin.

It's when my eyes dart to our surroundings that I suddenly spot it. "Over there," I exclaim as I find the green hammock attached to the trees. "We found it, Kellan. We did it."

Kellan sighs in relief while I instinctively tighten my grip on the straps of my backpack with excitement. I've packed our drinks and other necessities for us to have a relaxing time in the hammock. This does look like a perfect getaway.

When we reach the hammock, I put my backpack down and drop on my knee to check our stuff, but the moment I can't find the books we're going to read together, my heart sinks.

"Oh, God."

"What?" Kellan frowns, sounding alarmed.

"I forgot to bring the new books I bought for us. I think I left it in the cabin." I snap my palm on my forehead, squeezing my eyes shut.

I'm so stupid.

How could I forget? I was such in a hurry.

He sighs. "Wait here." He's about to turn around when I grab his arm.

"No. Where are you going?"

"Getting the books," he says like it's the most obvious thing in the world.

Quickly, I shake my head in disagreement. It's stupid because he can't see me.

"I'll go get it," I say. "Just wait for me here."

Kellan looks doubtful, but I'm sure that I should be the one doing it. He's the one who led the way here, but having no sight will trouble him again, especially since he hasn't completely readjusted to the surroundings here.

"Trust me," I urge. "I remember the way. I'll be back in no time."

Before he can complain, I rush back to the cabin, running through the woods. It's actually not a difficult path to follow because the ground where we stepped on looks like it's been walked on countless times. The hammock I saw just now is still pretty decent and in good condition despite the long years of not being used, so I guess that the cleaner Jackson paid takes care of it regularly.

Once I reach the cabin, I rush into the bedroom and find the books I was planning to pack still lying on the bed. I curse myself for my stupidity. It's when I snatch them that I hear the sound of water dropping against the roof.

I snap my head toward the window and find that it's starting to rain.

Oh, God. Kellan.

My heart beats faster, knowing that it's his fear to be in the rain.

Unfortunately, when I step out of the cabin, the rain has poured even harder.

No, please. Not now.

My boots stomp the ground when I make my way back to the hammock. My pulse quickens. I pant nervously as the rain falls extremely harshly.

I'm soaked from head to toe, and I have to stop because I suddenly can't see anything due to how hard it's raining. The water runs down my face rapidly, and I blink a few times to regain my sight.

Thunder strikes, making me jump. My chest heaves up and down as my teeth start to chatter because of the coldness. I'm trying my best to find my way to the hammock, but it's so damn difficult because suddenly everything around me looks the same.

"Kellan," I shout at the top of my lungs, but the sound of the harsh rain muffles my voice.

This. This is exactly what Kellan fears.

And he's alone now. I have to find him. Fast.

My worry for him escalates. I run faster, blindly. I can feel what he's feeling, as though our soul is the same.

Fear consumes me when I continue to look for him like a panicked deer in the forest.

"Kellan." My throat hurts because of screaming his name.

Just when I feel like bursting into tears, I find him.

Standing alone in the middle of the woods and pouring rain.

He freezes on the spot, as though he can't even move an inch.

My shaky legs bring me closer to him, and when I touch his arms, I notice that his whole body is trembling.

I pull him into a tight hug and cry, "Oh, God. I found you, Kellan. I found you. I'm here."

He's still not moving, and I tighten my hold on him like my life depends on him.

I'd never been this worried about someone.

The rain keeps pouring down on us. It's cold, and I embrace him even more in my arms. I want to make him warm although it feels like an impossible task. I wish I could transfer all the warmth in my body, just to save him. I don't care if I'm the one left in coldness.

Slowly, Kellan starts to move his arms. Even though he's still shaking all over, he wraps his arms around me. Relief washes over me, and my tears mingle with the rain streaming down my face.

"It's okay. It's all right. I'm right here," I rasp.

He tightens his grip around my body, and I bury my face in his chest.

The sound of the woods being burned inside the fireplace fills the room. Kellan and I are wrapped in a blanket. We're sitting in front of the fireplace.

The heat has made us stop shivering, and my heart has started calming down. We've tossed our drenched clothes, but we're not naked. I've changed into a pair of pajamas, and Kellan is wearing shorts.

I look up at Kellan, who's staring in the direction of the fire. His side view -- hit by the light emitting from the flame in this dim-lit room -- is perfect. I wonder how someone could have such perfect features.

I can see the reflection of the fire dancing in his mesmerizing grey eyes, and I wish that I could capture this beautiful sight.

"What are you thinking about?" I whisper.

He doesn't answer for a long moment, but then he says, "I don't know. Everything."

My brows furrow. I hug my knees tighter, leaning closer to him under the blanket. "Tell me," I say gently.

He still doesn't shift his gaze to me. "I want you to be happy, Layla."

My frown grows deeper as I wonder what's on his mind. I shake my head, and a small smile touches my lips. "I am," I say without any ounce of doubt. "Especially now. I'm happy being here with you."

I hear nothing from him, so I touch his cheek, making him turn his head toward me.

"Are you?" I ask, staring into his eyes and hoping to see the light in them again. I think that I'm seeing it now, but I can't be sure because Kellan rarely smiles.

"Here with you?" he asks.

I wait for him to say more. I'm dying to know his answer.

"You have no idea," he speaks through clenched teeth.

I wish he could just give me a yes or no answer because his words confuse me. Yet, deep in my heart, I know the answer.

"Kiss me," I whisper, wanting him to erase any doubt I have in my mind.

I'll find the answer again in the way he kisses me. I found it before.

Kellan's face draws closer to mine, and I close my eyes. His lips brush against mine, and I feel my heart burst.

He moves his lips on mine, slowly, carefully, like I'm a fragile thing that he can break at any time. But then, his chest starts to rise and fall. His breathing becomes quicker, like he can't hold the emotions building up inside him.

He kisses me more urgently, with such passion. I can't help but touch his chest. I need to feel him more. I need him.

He shudders as my fingers graze his bare chest. He puts his hand on my nape, deepening our kiss. Then he licks my lower lip, asking for permission. When I give it to him, he caresses my tongue with his. I moan, and it sounds so vulnerable, echoing in the silent room.

The temperature seems to increase significantly, and I know that it's not because of the fireplace next to us.

Kellan travels his hand upward to my hair. He gently runs his fingers through it before he suddenly grabs a fistful of it. He tilts my neck to the side, and the next thing I feel is his butterfly kisses along my neck.

My moans are now mixed with gasps. I'm burning from his touch. My lips part as I close my eyes. I want to feel him more, and more.

"Fuck," he curses under his breath before returning his lips to mine.

I arch, wrapping my arms around his neck and settling myself on his lap. His hands caress my back and waist -- I can even feel his fingers slipping under my pajama top to feel the skin on my back.

"Layla," he warns.

But I can't think clearly.

We kiss, kiss, and kiss like we need each other to breathe.

Kellan gasps as I unknowingly grind my hips against his. The next thing I feel is being pushed backward until my back lies on the wooden floor with a thud.

My eyes snap open, only to find Kellan towering over me with hunger in his eyes. He secures my wrists with one hand and places them above my head.

I enjoyed touching him with my hands, but I would be lying if I said that his dominance didn't turn me on.

He's panting, and I am too.

"I'm sorry. I can't," he says in a painful whisper.

I can only stare at him with a lost expression.

"I really can't. I'm not ready to take it further." He shuts his eyes in frustration. "It fucking hurts."

I can hear his ragged breathing. I wonder what is wrong because he indeed looks like he's in pain. Worry stirs my insides. I wait in silence as he tries to compose himself.

Kellan opens his eyes again, and the look he gives me is so intense. He slowly guides my hand to touch his chest, and when my palm is placed over his heart, I can feel how hard it's thumping. It's crazy. It feels like it's about to burst out of his chest.

He swallows, keeping his hold on my wrist to make me feel his heartbeat longer.

"This is why I can't do it," he says in a hoarse voice. "I'm blind, but my other senses are overwhelming when it comes to you. My heart is about to explode every time we touch, every time I feel your skin on mine, your lips on mine, your breath against my skin, your moans in my ear. Fuck. Layla, I can't fucking control my heart if you do that to me."

He's literally shaking, and tears pool in my eyes.

I never thought that our closeness would be too overwhelming to him because of his heightened senses. I felt that my heart was about to burst, but I didn't know that his was even worse.

"I'm sorry." I swallow. "I shouldn't have..." I falter, stumbling upon my words.

I feel flattered and embarrassed at the same time.

"I should have known that you were not ready," I say.

Kellan sighs. I sit up, watching him stare down at the floor. There's a blush creeping on his cheeks, and I just can't resist the urge to hug him.

I circle my arms around his neck and bury my face in his nape. "Just a hug. I promise."

A few seconds pass in silence before he whispers, "Okay."

28

CHAPTER 28

L AYLA

Today, we finally manage to spend time in the hammock after we didn't make it the other day because of the rain.

The hammock is quite spacious. It can fit four people, so Kellan and I can lie on it comfortably with still enough space to stretch our legs. I'm now lying on my back and staring at the blue sky above. Kellan is right next to me, hugging my shoulder.

I rest my head on his shoulder blade, smiling softly. It feels so peaceful here. The birds are chirping above us, enjoying this beautiful forest as well.

"Can you tell me what you feel about this woods?" I ask.

"Hm?"

"I know that you can feel everything," I say, "and you can know what's happening around you by using your other senses. I want to know."

"Birds," he says with amusement because it's just so obvious.

"How many?" I grin.

"Three. At least, they're the ones who are not shy to stop at the branches just above us," he jokes.

I gaze at the birds. He's correct. There are three of them, and I don't know how he does that. Maybe he can even feel their movement.

"Wait." Kellan suddenly sits up.

My curiosity kicks in. I sit up too.

"I think one of them is flirting with the other," he suddenly says.

I can't help but laugh. "You're impossible." I push his chest playfully.

"No, listen." He puts his finger over his mouth, and my laughter stops short. "Can't you hear that?" he asks as I watch the birds again. "One of them keeps fluttering their wings to attract their mate."

My eyes widen as I find out that he's right.

"See?" he says, still with the same amusement glinting in his eyes. "I think it's a male, fluffing out his feathers. Usually, the male ones will dance to begin the courtship. Fuck. He's going to do it."

I watch as the third bird suddenly flies away. "That one doesn't want to be the third wheel." A burst of laughter leaves my mouth again.

I gaze up at them while one of them is indeed doing fantastic dancing to attract the other. I can't help but giggle because it's such a fun and interesting thing to watch.

When the dance is over, I ask, "Now what?"

Kellan looks like he's in deep thought. "I don't know. Judging from the sound of his legs starting to get restless against the branch, I think that he can't wait to fly away."

To my surprise, the bird does just as Kellan expects. He flies away but is then followed by the female one.

"Where are they going?" I ask curiously.

Kellan shrugs. "Some birds build their nests for their mates. Maybe he's showing her the nests to let her choose."

My mouth hangs open in amazement. "I hope they get their happily ever after," I say giddily.

It's just a simple story about what happens to the wild lives around us, but witnessing it brings me so much joy. To be able to enjoy the simple things in life is a blessing.

Kellan tilts his chin up at the trees above us. He stares up at the sky, crossing his legs and resting his elbows on each of his knees. The corner of his mouth curves into a small smile while the wind blows his hair softly. There's only contentment in his expression, and this beautiful sight makes my breath catch in my throat.

I take out my phone and secretly snap a picture of him. I think that he can feel it because he then diverts his eyes to me.

"Did you just secretly take a picture of me?"

I chuckle. "What if I did?"

Had this happened when I met him for the first time, I would have thought that I was tottering on dangerous grounds by secretly taking pictures of the heir of Black Wings.

But now, the man who used to give me a menacing look only shakes his head in disbelief.

Kellan lies back in the hammock. I take out my book from my backpack and lie next to him, snuggling up to him.

"Should we read the book again?" I ask.

"Yeah," he whispers. "I like it when you read to me."

I begin to read the poetry book. My voice echoes, mixed with the sound of the rustling leaves blown by the wind and the birds chirping again above us.

I keep reading, unaware that the atmosphere slowly lulls me to sleep. My voice is getting softer and softer the longer time passes.

"They should feel like home..." I falter. My eyes feel so heavy. "A place that..." I can't even continue the sentence because I start to doze off.

The last thing I feel is Kellan's kiss on my forehead.

Kellan and I are lying on the bed, facing each other. I wrap my arms around his waist while he pulls me closer to him. His hand is on my back, over the fabric of my sleep shirt. The other hand caresses my head while I bury my face in his chest.

I inhale his scent, feeling safe and secure in his arms. These past few days in the cabin have been like a dream that I don't want to wake up to.

I wish that we could stay like this forever.

"What's your dream, Layla?" he suddenly asks. "What do you want to be in the future?"

My dream is right here with you. I want to answer that, but the latter question makes me realize that he's actually asking about something more accurate.

"I don't know," I say. "I haven't applied to any college because I thought that I wouldn't be able to afford it."

I remember exactly why I accepted the job Jaxon gave me.

I never thought that it would turn into something like this.

With the money Jaxon already transferred to my account, I will have no problem helping my family financially and applying for college. But I don't want to leave just yet. In fact, I don't think that I'll ever want to leave Kellan.

"What do you enjoy the most?" He tucks a strand of my hair behind my ear.

I stare into his beautiful grey eyes, drowning in them.

"Maybe it can help you choose your major," he says.

I sigh, closing my eyes as I shake my head. I lean into his chest even closer, my fingers gripping the back of his t-shirt.

"I don't know," I say. "I like giving help to people, though. I honestly thought of becoming a nurse or being involved in a volunteer program for kids somewhere in the world," I pause. "Why are you suddenly asking me about that?"

I tilt my chin up and see Kellan giving me a serious look.

"Don't you have a plan for your future?" he asks softly.

Now that he asks me, I honestly haven't thought about it in detail.

I shake my head again. "I haven't thought about it specifically. What I'm sure about is that I want to help Nana and my brother, Archer, financially--"

My brows furrow as I think hard about what I'm going to do in the future. I don't think that I'll be able to live like a normal person now that I'm a part of Black Wings, so I don't understand why Kellan is asking me these questions.

"Hey, what's wrong?" he whispers.

When I look at him again, I see the concern on his face.

"Never mind." I chuckle softly.

He tilts my chin up again with his finger and gives me a soft kiss on the lips. I sigh in contentment and push my body against him.

This time, I initiate the kiss, circling my arm around his neck. I move my mouth against his and suck his bottom lip, earning his gasp. He immediately tightens his hold on me, wrapping his arms around me possessively and starting to kiss me hungrily.

I kiss him back with all my heart, and before I know it, we are burning with passion and desire. Our tongues dance with each other as I wrap my leg around his waist. He groans, and the next thing I know is that he flips me onto my back.

He locks my hands on my sides, his jaw tight. "Layla," he growls, warning me.

"I'm sorry." I gulp. "Sorry."

His eyes soften, and then he releases me. I lay on my side, facing the opposite direction.

Again, I pushed him too far.

I scold myself for how stupid I am. Kellan is not ready yet for that kind of intimacy.

I feel him moving behind me and spooning me. He rests his chin on my shoulder, and I smile.

"Cuddling time?" I tease. "Okay. Cuddling only."

"You're going to be the death of me," he mutters under his breath and places a soft kiss on my neck.

I sigh dreamily, feeling him placing more kisses on the back of my neck.

"Kellan." I giggle. "It tickles."

But he doesn't stop, and more giggles burst from me.

29

Chapter 29

LAYLA

I squeeze my eyes, feeling the ray of morning sun hitting my face. When I open them, I'm greeted by the familiar cabin I've been staying in with Kellan for these past few days.

I turn my head to my side and find that his side of the bed is empty. When I graze my fingers on the sheet, it feels cold. I frown.

Kellan must have left the bed for quite a while.

"Kellan?" I call, my voice still groggy from sleep.

I sit up, stretch, and get out of the bed. I walk slowly toward the living room and find that it's empty. The curtain moves, blown by the soft morning breeze, but other than that, there's no sign of any other movement.

I wonder where Kellan is, but then a soft smile touches my lips. He usually sits at the back patio in the morning if he wakes up earlier than I do. I shake my head in disbelief due to my own cluelessness.

Maybe it's because he was holding me tight all night that I expected him to be by my side when I opened my eyes -- he acted like he didn't even want to let me go for a second when we slept together last night.

I step onto the patio, only to find that it's deserted as well. My brows furrow in confusion.

Is it possible that he's taking a morning jog?

But he never did that during our time here -- he was still traumatized after what Marco's brother did to me.

"Kellan?" I call again, rushing back into the living room.

I push through the front door, only to be greeted by the deserted lawn.

My worry escalates. Where could he possibly go?

He hasn't been fully familiar with the surroundings outside the cabin.

Unless he went to the hammock.

My thought leads me there, and my legs bring me closer to the woods even before I remember moving them. I follow the path toward the hammock. My heart is racing.

When I finally reach the spot, I'm already panting.

He's not here.

My pulse quickens even more. I rush back toward the cabin, worrying about Kellan.

Is he in the bathroom? But everything has been so silent, I don't even think that he's here with me.

I run into the cabin and knock on the bathroom door. "Kellan, are you there?"

No answer.

With my heart thumping hard against my rib cage, I open the door. It's not locked, and when I look inside, no one is there.

My lips start to tremble because of the sudden horrible feeling stirring in my heart.

I step back into the bedroom, and my eyes land on my phone, which is lying on the nightstand.

He couldn't possibly leave without letting me know, so he must have contacted me.

With a heavy heart, I take my phone from the nightstand, and on the screen, there it is.

A voice message from him.

Everything around me seems to stop. My curiosity kicks in, but a part of me screams to not open that message because it will be something that I don't ever want to hear.

With my shaking hand, I press the button to listen to what he had to say to me. His voice fills the air, and I can already feel the tears welling up in my eyes before I even hear him speaking.

"Hey, Layla. I'm sorry. I had to go. I asked Stas to pick me up before it reached dawn because I didn't want to wake you up. I knew that I couldn't do it if you saw me leaving."

He takes a deep breath, and it's shaky.

"I just wanted to say that I really enjoyed what we had. The times we spent in the cabin were the best moments of my life, and I will never forget that. Thank you for being there for me when I needed it. Uh... I don't know where to start because there are so many things I want to say to you, and I don't think that my words will be enough to tell you how much I feel for you.

You came, and I wasn't ready to accept a person like you in my life. You stayed, and you annoyed the hell out of me because being near you made me feel a lot of things...things that I didn't expect I would feel. I was trying so hard to deny you, and I'm so sorry."

His voice cracks, and he takes another deep breath.

"You taught me a lot of things. You spoke as if I could also see all the beautiful things you saw. And goddammit, Layla, I could see. I could see them when I was with you. I could enjoy all the little things in life, and I'm addicted to you. I can hear your beauty, and I can feel everything about you -- your happiness, your fear and your sadness."

He turns silent and sniffs.

"I told you that I was not your hero, but I wanted to be, more than anything else in the world. So, I'm going to ask you to let me be. Let me protect you. Let me free you from any harm. Let me help you follow your dreams and have a happy life. I want you to be happy, Layla, and I have to let you go."

He chokes on his words.

"Black Wings is not for you. It's only for me. It's in my blood, where I belong. But it's not for you. You're not going to be there anymore because you deserve so much more. Live your life, Layla. See more of its beauty. For yourself. And for me."

When the message ends, tears are streaming down my face. Hard.

I grip my chest because of how painful it feels. The phone falls from my hold, clattering on the ground.

"You can't--" I choke on my sobs. "You can't do this, Kellan."

He won't let us be together. He's doing this for me, but my heart is already shattered so badly that I don't even think it will ever heal without him by my side.

My cries echo in the room, and I'm already longing for the man with the purest heart I've ever known, with the most beautiful and kindest eyes I've ever seen.

The man who would do anything to protect me.

I quickly dial his number. I need to talk to him again, to hear his voice again and make sure that he didn't mean all of this.

"The number you have called is no longer in service."

My sobs break even more. "No." My lips tremble as I taste my own tears. "Please, Kellan. I need to see you again."

I swallow a lump in my throat. It hurts so much to the point that it's hard to breathe.

Kellan has let me go.

And his last wish for me to fulfill is to let him be my hero, in his own unselfish way.

30

Epilogue

One year later

LAYLA

"Over here, Layla," my friend's voice calls me as soon as I step into the coffee shop.

My eyes dart to her waving her hand enthusiastically. She's sitting with two of our other classmates.

A smile forms on my lips as I walk toward their table with my backpack slung across my shoulder. I take a seat and take out my laptop.

Naomi -- who just waved her hand at me -- squints at me, resting her chin on her fist. "Are you not going to order something first?" She tilts her chin toward the counter.

I shake my head. "I'm good." I usually take my coffee outside.

"I'm sure we can finish our assignment quickly today," Kenna, who is sitting beside me, mumbles and slurps her iced coffee. "Now that Layla is here, of course. Gosh, you're our life safer, Layla."

I almost roll my eyes. A small chuckle leaves my lips. She's hyperbolizing.

"No, really," Sofie adds. "You're always one step ahead when it comes to studying. How the hell did you manage to get a high mark for our last quiz? Our professor is a pain in the ass."

"That's what happens when you're really passionate about what you're studying," Naomi chirps, raising her brow at me. "Right, Layla?"

I shake my head, biting my lip as I try to focus on our assignment instead. Studying nutrition is indeed my passion. Many kids around the world -- especially those who stay in poor countries -- are struggling to have proper food, and I'm looking forward to participating in a volunteer program to help them.

I smile as I remember being told to make the most out of my life, and to be happy.

We do our assignments while chatting about nothing important in particular. I must admit that I enjoy being here with them. I even enjoy the bickering between Sofie and Kenna as well as Naomi's ramble.

Being a college girl, pursuing the degree of my dreams, and hanging out with my friends after class have been my daily routines. The money from Jaxon is more than enough to cover all of Nana's insurance debt, the tuition for Archer's school as well as the expenses I need to pursue higher education.

I can't be more grateful although there's still a big hole in my chest that I doubt will ever be fulfilled.

We manage to finish the group assignment quite quickly, just as Kenna predicted. I'm really glad about that because I have to leave early to celebrate Archer's birthday.

While they're still packing their things before leaving, I head to the counter to order. After grabbing my favorite cappuccino, I sling my backpack over my shoulder and wave at them. "I gotta go. It's my brother's birthday celebration today."

"Safe trip."

"Call me when you get there."

"Have a nice long weekend, Layla."

They say almost in unison, and I smile at them before pushing through the door.

The autumn breeze greets me as soon as I step out of the coffee shop. I take a moment to halt and close my eyes, enjoying the feel of it caressing my skin.

I resume my steps and head toward the tunnel, but not before I pass the park where I usually sit and enjoy the sunset while listening to the kids playing in the playground.

A soccer ball almost shoots my drink, but luckily, I manage to dodge it with a little yelp.

The boy who just kicked the ball runs toward me. "Sorry," he shouts from afar, rushing here.

I smile and pick up the ball rolling beside my foot. I throw it at him, and he catches it with a wide grin on his face.

"Thanks," he says.

The boy is cute and still so little, probably not more than five years old.

I sigh, walking closer toward the playground. I lean against the railing, watching the kids play as I slurp my cappuccino. I moan as the warmth of the drink sips into me. Even the warmth of the cup against my palm feels so nice and relaxing.

My gaze darts to a little girl playing the swing with her father. The children's laughter echoes in my ears, and I unknowingly let another smile curve on my lips. It's always heartwarming to watch them play. I don't think that I'll ever get bored of it.

I turn around, and just when I head to the bench, I see Mr Grint -- the old man who cleans the park -- working with his broom to sweep the leaves off the pavements and the grass. He spots me too.

I wave my hand at him and call cheerfully, "Hi Mr Grint."

"Enjoying the sunset again?" he asks with his signature grandpa's voice.

"As usual." I grin.

He nods and resumes his work again. Mr Grint is everybody's best friend here.

I take a seat in my favorite spot, still holding the cup of coffee with both hands. I close my eyes and inhale the soothing aroma. Doing this always calms my mind.

I open my eyes again and stare at the sky. It's twilight. The setting sun is hidden by the buildings, but it's still a beautiful sight to see. Purple, red, and orange.

How I wish that I could show this view to him. The person I miss the most. The man with no sight, but the one who also said that I could give him his sight every time he was with me.

My throat starts to hurt because of the great longing I feel inside. Slowly, I take out my phone from my pants and find his picture. It's a picture of him when he sat in the hammock, gazing up at the surroundings with a contented expression and a smile that rarely touched his lips.

My eyes water as I stare at the light in his eyes -- his happiness -- that I want to treasure forever. I miss that face.

I miss him.

So much.

My tear drops onto the screen, and I wipe my eye. I always think about him.

Is he doing okay?

Does he still have that light in him?

I sniffle, glancing at my wristwatch. It's about time for me to catch the train. Nana and Archer are waiting for me.

With that thought in mind, I put my phone back into my pocket and finish the remaining of my drink with my eyes glued to the beautiful twilight sky.

KELLAN

I walk along the pavement, using the hoodie on my sweater to cover my hair and face.

It would be bad if my enemy knew that I was walking around, and it would be even worse if that happened while Layla was here.

I step into the park and immediately know that Mr Grint is waiting for me. The sweeping sound of his broom stops short the moment I enter the site. I hear his boots stepping closer to me.

"She has left," he says as I halt. "She had to catch the train."

I nod.

One would think that he's just an old man who cleans the park, but the truth is that he's a part of Black Wings. He's close to my family. We trust him to take care of the cabin near the lake. That place holds so many memories for my family, and now it's even more special because of my time with Layla there.

"She's doing good," Mr Grint says. "Safe. No stalker. Other than you, of course."

I listen as he tells me more about Layla -- how she spent her day, if she sounded happy, her friends, and if there's anything that I should worry about.

Another relief washes over me as I know that she's doing okay.

"She still sheds tears because of you," he tells me in a warning tone.

I swallow a lump in my throat. I don't want her to forget about me, but on the other hand, I don't want her to cry. I've been telling myself to wait for the day when she moves on and forgets about me.

Mr Grint pats my shoulder, and I resume my steps to walk toward the coffee shop.

I push through the door, and the smell of coffee strikes my nostrils. It's the smell I love because it feels close to her.

I can sense the customers snapping their heads toward me when I open the door. I silently curse. I don't know if it's the fact that I'm taller than most people or my emotionless face makes people cower, but I definitely attract attention whenever I walk. This hoodie is not fucking doing its job, and it pisses me off.

Mr Grint's words echo back in my head, and the next thing I know is that I'm following her shadow.

"One cappuccino," I say my order to the barista.

I heard that Layla went to this coffee shop after her class and ordered a cup of hot cappuccino.

I heard that she chatted with her friends here, having a great time.

I close my eyes, waiting for my coffee to be ready. I hear the sound of people talking inside the cafe, the clattering glasses, the drinks being mixed on the counter, and the bustling sound of college students going in and out.

The things she heard.

I open my eyes when the barista hands me the drink, and for a moment, I breathe the aroma of her favorite drink.

I could almost hear her sigh of contentment, her voice when she talked to her friends, and her laughter when she heard something funny.

The warmth of the liquid inside the cup sips into my palm as I head back toward the door. It's something that I find comforting.

I step outside, feeling the breeze blowing through my skin. My chest tightens because of this overwhelming feeling inside me. It's the air she breathes, and it makes me feel her. Everywhere.

She's with me, sharing her joy, until I can't feel my anger anymore.

While I'm walking back toward the park, I hear the sound of children playing, the sound of the swing, and the kick of a ball. My heart warms at the thought of her smiling when she watched them.

I take a seat on the bench and slurp my coffee. A sigh leaves my lips. It tastes bitter and sweet. Just like us.

I miss her, the girl who gave me another sight after I lost one. This sight she gave me makes me feel whole.

The breeze caresses my skin again, as if it's trying to soothe the pain of missing her.

A tear falls from my eye, and a shaky breath escapes from my mouth.

I love her. I can feel her everywhere.

I love Layla Hayes, and I don't need my eyes to see her.